A Darker Moon

A DARKER MOON

J. S. Watts

Vagabondage Press

A Darker Moon

© 2012 by J.S. Watts

ISBN-13: 978-0615706528
ISBN-10: 0615706525

Vagabondage Press
PO Box 3563
Apollo Beach, Florida 33572
http://www.vagabondagepress.com

First edition printed in the United States of America and the United Kingdom, October 2012

10 9 8 7 6 5 4 3 2

Cover images by Vladimir Vitek and James Knopf. Cover design by Maggie Ward.

A Darker Moon

For all my boys

1

A small brown owl perches on my cot rail, its huge, yellow eyes like two full harvest moons. It may only be a little owl, but those eyes are big enough to drown an infant, and I have a sense of falling, of being sucked in and down towards two pools of deep moonlight. It is my earliest memory.

It is followed very closely, within the variable flow of remembered time, by another in which an elderly woman, whom retrospectively I have assumed to be one of my many carers, taps my lips with an ungentle finger and mutters unintelligible mantras, unintelligible that is, except for one word, "Lilith." That word and the two luminous drowning pools imprinted themselves on my consciousness and haunted me into adulthood. Even now, I sometimes wake with a start from a dream in which I am forever falling to hear the fading hiss of a whispered "Lilith," convinced I have been listening to mumbled septuagenarian incantations in my sleep. As for owls, they have a morbid fascination for me, but I couldn't bear to live within the sound of their call.

I think it is fair to say that I did not have a settled childhood and most of my different carers and foster homes have become something of an amorphous blur in the mental album of my recollections. In addition to the early memories, the only other strong image I have from this first period of my life is of my mother, or rather, of the one and only photograph that I have of her.

I do not actually remember my mother. When she abandoned me in a basket on the steps of a North London synagogue, the only things she left me with were barely enough blankets, my first name (written on the back of an address card of a less than reputable Soho nightclub of the time), and a black and white photograph of herself. At least everyone, including me, has always assumed that it is a photograph of her. There is no name or inscription on the photo, or any other indication as to whom it is. But why would you leave a photograph of just anyone with an abandoned baby; it must be my mother. It *has* to be her.

In the photograph, she is standing partially side on to the camera with her face turned to look at the photographer. She holds her hands behind her back. And in them is something dark, it is not clear what: a clutch bag or a book, maybe? Perhaps she was studious. Her hair is long, black, and gently wavy. She is wearing it loose and slightly unkempt. Her dark eyes stare directly at the camera, her face unsmiling, but not stern; more quietly confident, mildly challenging, maybe a trifle arrogant. Wearing a long baggy dress and beads, a feather boa draped around her neck and with her tousled hair, she looks like a hippy, a sixties love-child. Sometimes, I wonder if I was the real love-child: a freebie that came with the free love of the era; an unexpected and unasked for acquisition that she felt equally free to give away and pass on without compunction or guilt. On days when I am feeling somewhat more generous towards her, I wonder if she was a working girl, hence the nightclub card, who fell on hard times and gave me up, with tears and regrets, in order to give me a better life than she could offer. Who knows? I certainly don't, but at least I have the freedom to create stories that shine a little light on the gloomier and more uncertain parts of my life.

Of my father I know even less: no name, no photograph, no nothing. My hair and eye colour are dark like the woman's in the photograph. Does that mean my father was equally dark, or just that my mother's were the stronger genes of the two?

The fact that I know nothing of my father does not bother me. The little information I have about my mother, as constructed from her possible photograph, gnaws away at me, but over the years I have had to learn to deal with the bite marks.

Yet another unknown aspect of my heritage is my faith: Am I Jewish? My mother had dark hair and eyes and abandoned me at a synagogue; little enough to go on, but it might indicate a Hebrew legacy, mightn't it? I, too, am dark-haired and dark-eyed and my name is Old Testament kosher, though I am not circumcised. This gave the rabbi who found me, like a land-locked, latter-day Moses, something of a dilemma: Should he hand over full responsibility for me to the secular authorities, or ensure I was brought up as one of the chosen people? It would have been nice to have been chosen. My maybe-mother looked as if she might have been Jewish, which should have counted for something, but there was no way of telling. I had been found on a Friday, just at sunset, so the rabbi kept me for the Sabbath and then handed me over, lock, stock and blankets, to Social Services as soon as possible the following Monday morning, and I do mean as soon as possible. One of my old social workers told me he was standing on the department steps, with me and the basket thrust down at his feet, well before anyone had arrived at the office to open up.

From this inauspicious start in life I entered the state care system as a doubly rejected child of unknown parentage and indeterminate faith, with only a set of poor quality blankets, an anonymous photograph, and a card from the disreputable Black Moon Club to my name.

I have other memories; some quite vivid. Those that I can place chronologically, I have built into the story of my childhood. That will come later. But, there are memories I cannot locate in time, cannot anchor to a *there* or *then*, or anything that flows with the current of my story.

"*Bastard! Got no mummy. Got no daddy. You're a bastard. Bar. Stud.*"

"*I'm not.*"

"*No mummy. No daddy. Bastard. Bastard.*"

"*I've got a mummy. I've got a mummy. I have.*"

I had. I have.

Then there was the cat.

She was little more than a kitten, really, silky black fur, a white line down her nose, little white paws, and she was mine. She adopted me. She took titbits from my fingers and purred when I came near. Then I heard him.

"Evie. Evie. Come here, Evie."

"She won't come to you."

"Yes she will. Evie, come here, Evie."

"She won't come to you. She's mine, and she's not called Evie."

"She's not yours. She's not anybody's, and if I want to call her Evie, I can."

"Can't."

"Can."

"Can't."

"What do you call her?"

"I don't."

"Then I can call her what I like. Evie, come here, Evie."

And she came. To him. She took food from out of his hand. And she purred.

I never fed her after that. If she came after me, I threw stones at her. Some hit her. She yowled. She never bothered me again

I can also remember books. Rows and rows of them. Stacks. A library. Old and dusty. Were they mine? No one else seemed interested in them, so they can't have been very valuable. I can't remember what was in them, what they were about. What was the value of them? Only what I remember.

And finally, candles. Rows and rows of them, too. Lighting the way down the steps: steep, made of stone, going all the way down into the blackness at the bottom. Dark, moist, waiting.

"You dream of candles. You're weird."

"No I'm not."

"Weird boy. Weird boy."

"I'm not weird. It's only a dream. Everybody dreams."

"Weird boy, weirdy boy, beardy boy, bastard. Got no mummy nor no daddy. Bastard. Barst. Ud."

"I'm not. I've got a mummy. I have. I have. I've seen her picture. She's mine."

III

Welcome to my childhood. Whilst it was unsettled, it was not especially unhappy, at least not in the way of child chimney sweeps or the two little princes in the Tower. Yes, I had upsets, but I learned to adapt, to get on with life. I became good at mixing with all sorts of people, irrespective of background; I had none to speak of myself, so why should I care about it in regards to others? I learnt to socialise whenever I had the opportunity and to value my own company when I did not. Above all, I acquired resilience, self reliance, and the knack of spinning an entertaining tale: all necessary survival skills in the constant shuttling back and forth between foster placements and care homes that marked the formative years of my life.

To this day, I do not fully understand what led to my inability to find a proper home and turned me into the human equivalent of a ricocheting ping pong ball. I was abandoned as a small baby, usually enough in itself to result in a scramble of potential adopters; babies are attractive take-home prospects in a way that tantrum throwing toddlers, boisterous children, and bolshie, angst-ridden teenagers are not. The few photographs I have of me show a cute baby and a handsome enough child. Yet, somehow I was never wanted enough, never chosen. All my foster placements were strikingly short-lived and a pattern rapidly developed in terms of any attempt at finding a real home for me.

Things would always start encouragingly. I would arrive at the home of the potential adoptive or foster parents without mishap. After the warm welcomes, I would begin the process of bedding down into my new location. All would be going well. There would be positive reports about my good behaviour, no signs of any disruptive or alarming tendencies, and my health would be commendably sound. Then, the problems would start. Looking back over my records, once I was able to gain access to them, the first signs would be reports of disrupted sleep, initially for me and then spreading to all other members of the family. I can't remember any of this. Clearly, I wouldn't whilst still a baby, but the same happened well into my childhood. Yet each time, while I apparently remained content, my host family's contentment rapidly waned.

"He's having one of those weird dreams, I'm telling you."

"Everybody dreams."

"Yeah, but not like this."

Next would come reports of nighttime disturbances, abnormally distressing nightmares (and not just mine), sleepwalking, screaming in my sleep and vague references to troubled nocturnal behaviour. People seemed to struggle to articulate the nature of the problems, but they were adamant they existed. I, however, was blissfully unaware of the nighttime chaos around me. Indeed, that seemed to be part of the problem. People would try to talk to me about what was happening, and I would have no recollection of anything. Once old enough, I would usually deny it, claiming I was perfectly happy and enjoying my stay. Apparently, though, nobody else was. The trouble was, whilst I denied there was an issue, or was unable (or unwilling) to talk about it, there was no hope of remedy or firm corrective action (the approach depending on my hosts' point of view). Sometimes the social work reports would record a crescendo of disruption with things getting accidentally broken, or wanton after-dark vandalism (again depending on the viewpoint of the report's author). But, in any event, it would not be long before things reached metaphorical, if not actual, breaking point, and inevitably it was back to the children's home, unwanted yet again.

Whatever unconscious or subconscious issues were plaguing my abortive placements, the symptoms apparently stopped as soon as I arrived back at the institution. The home would monitor me on my return, but my nighttimes remained resolutely problem free. The early reports on my infant placements made none too subtle comments about the stability or over sensitivity of the host families, but eventually, even Social Services recognised a pattern, however unusual, and could not keep blaming the matter entirely on the receiving household. The none too subtle comments started to be directed at me.

"*Back again, boy? What did you do this time?*"

Therapy was attempted, but, as I kept insisting that everything was okay and was sleeping well when at the children's home, it was difficult even for professionals to know where to begin. Talking therapies obviously wouldn't work, neither did play therapy. They still tried, though. How they tried.

"*You can compact a lifetime into the first seven years, you know, but it'll take the rest of your life to unpack it again.*"

Hypnotherapy and straightforward old-fashioned hypnotism were next up, but equally without success, and sleep monitoring produced no sign of issues whatsoever. I remained resolutely ignorant of what was allegedly taking place when I was on a placement, and so, by default, did my legal guardians. Even covertly monitoring my sleep when I was away from the institution failed to produce any sort of Jack-in-the-Box revelation, but put me on a placement without any monitoring, and the pattern soon re-established itself. Over the years, the length and number of placements grew less and less, whilst my time spent in formal childcare institutions grew.

At some stage in this serial melodrama, someone in Social Services wondered if my problem might be a cultural thing and suggested a foster placement within a reasonably Orthodox Jewish household, presumably in case my possibly Yiddish roots were not being properly nurtured. This placement turned out to be the most disastrous of all.

I can't drag up many memories from this time. I have tried. I have an image of a grey-haired, elderly couple, but all adults were elderly back then. I see them sitting drinking tea in the matron's office.

"*Hello, little man. How are we today?*"

"*Ah, just look at him. Such big eyes he's got.*"

Then I can see a house with a willow tree in the garden, a gloomy, shrub-lined front path, and a big wooden front door. It opens onto a long, dark hallway lined with shelves of books, so many books. I go on through the door, and the books surround me.

"Welcome to our house, young man. Be a good boy, and I'm sure you'll be happy here."

"Such a little dumpling. No, don't touch the books, there's a good boy."

Another placement had begun.

I can still smell the sickly antiseptic scent of Wright's Coal Tar soap and the separate allure of Jasmine. The soap was yellow, an uncomfortable acidic shade, the colour of mustard. I don't like mustard, and I never, ever, use Wright's Coal Tar. The smell alone is enough to make me gag. The Jasmine, however, was pure comfort: a scent of warm summer evenings and reassurance, a softness I wanted to sink myself down into like a deep feather pillow or thick, long hair.

Beyond that, I have little or no recollection of what actually took place, but my records show that phone calls about disrupted sleep started almost as soon as I had been put to bed in my putative new home. It did not take long for the calls to escalate and develop a hysterical edge. There were references to nocturnal noises, unacceptable night time behaviour, and filthy practices. The final discussions with Social Services, if discussion is indeed a viable term for the hysterical and rambling accusations reflected in my notes, make reference to matters in terms such as, "abomination," "cursed," and "demon child." I was only four. Social Services removed me immediately and gave up on any further overtly religious dimension to my placements.

Despite all this, I remember myself as being a remarkably content and placid child. I admit to some emotional scars, but the coping strategies I developed corrected, or at least masked, most of them. My Social Service guardians were surprised at how untroubled I remained. They never did fully believe the reports from the host families. The rest of the jury, however, was out — returning conflicting verdicts as to whether I was supremely unfortunate in the choice of foster parents or whether I was a lying, game-playing little shit, only once removed from the demon child described by Mr. and Mrs. Cohen. The latter theory gained increasing credibility as the number of abruptly terminated placements increased, but then, so presumably did the conviction that I was bad, not mad, and therefore unlikely to be damaged or troubled by yet another rejection. I, however, remained something of an innocent abroad, and my behaviour when not placed with a family was exemplary. I was always very good at doing what I was told. My care workers could not fault me and therefore had no knife to sharpen, even if they had wanted to. Life continued, and eventually thoughts of either adoption or fostering stopped all together, which was a shame: I would have liked to have been chosen.

I will pause here, just briefly, to let the memories embed themselves and be absorbed naturally into the flow of things. I am preparing the foundations. My present is built on my past, and its roots get everywhere.

May I ask you a question? Who are you and how do you know? Depending on who you think you are, you may understand the need for this pause, but then again, I must accept that you may not.

This isn't some old, faded story; this is my story, and once the story's done, what's left is just memory, all parts equal, the beginning as important as the ending. I didn't begin now. This is not who I am. *Then*, was who I am; *now* is only what I have become, and part of me believes I still don't have to accept it, that I still have a choice. Surely, the act of simply remaining alive means there are choices? How are you going to understand *now*, if you haven't seen *then*? How will you grasp *today*, if *yesterday* hasn't already grabbed you? Then, there is the trickier one: how does one ever seize the day, if the previous night still refuses to let go?

Yes, I can show you upfront where the owls fly and the river flows, black, silent and silky in the darkness, but what will it mean to you taken out of my life's context?

"Complicated? What do you mean by complicated?"

"It's because it fell sideways so it's neither one thing nor another."

"Kill him and have done with it. That's my choice."

I have learned there is a cost to being chosen. But, as to how much it actually costs…I guess that's just another question that's still waiting to be answered.

Briefly shining words, random flashes of light in a darkened room never seen before. Who knows when you will see it again? The dark is more confusing, the night blindness worse, because of the temporary illumination of those seemingly random flashes. Does it matter? To me it does — did — but I can't answer for the future. Maybe you can?

The light needs to burn through slowly, from the inside out, and you need to see things in a darker light to really make sense of their truths. I have lit the first wick, the first candle, on the journey forward, down into the open and waiting dark. The beginning of my story, or at least this story. My earliest signifiers.

And so the story continues…

The rest of my childhood was somewhat uneventful in comparison to the early years. Despite government statistics regarding children in care, I did well at school and then college. I was compliant. I enjoyed learning new things and showed a particular aptitude for English and creative writing. This, I put down to being a natural storyteller: a born onlooker.

Stories mattered. Initially, I told stories to make up for the obvious deficits in my family history, and indeed my family. I learned to create stories to explain away, to myself and the other children, my all too frequent returns to the institutional bosom. Stories were a way of making sense of an otherwise senseless world. Over the years my stories got better and more convincing, to the extent that I, at least, believed them. Storytelling was how I broke the ice with new people, made new friends. Stories were a way of constructing a positive sense of self. Let me explain. I'll tell you a story.

I must have been around twelve. A still-small, dark-haired boy in an ill-fitting blazer. I was at secondary school and doing surprisingly well. There was a school trip to a public art gallery: a largely futile attempt to introduce culture and creativity to the urban adolescent mind. Most of my classmates hated it, but I quite enjoyed myself. I liked the stories told by the pictures and not just by the paintings which recreated specific legends or events in history. I could just as easily find a tale hiding deep within a portrait or still life. I was happy wandering by myself around the exhibits, inventing lively dramas for their freeze-frame moments. I was particularly fascinated by the fact that faces from the early pictures (anything pre-Victorian as far as I was concerned) never seemed to resemble people alive today. In the later paintings, you could see faces you might meet on the bus or in the street in twentieth century London, but in the early stuff, people seemed to have arrived from another planet or be creatures from the myths and legends I enjoyed reading. I mean, could you imagine sitting opposite Gainsborough's Mr. Andrews or Dieric Bouts' man in red on a number 83 to Golders Green?

So there I was, rambling happily between paintings, drinking up the tales they offered, when I saw her. I think I was in the eighteenth century; certainly it was a period in which I did not expect to find real faces I could recognise. But here, hanging on a wall without warning, was a face I knew very well; I ought to, it was my mother. Except, of course, that it couldn't be, but it was the spitting image of her. Even the pose matched the one she had adopted in her photograph.

It was a full length portrait of someone called Lily. She was standing partially side on to the observer, but gazing straight at you with a challenging look in her dark brown eyes. She was wearing a midnight blue dress in the style of a Jane Austen heroine, or at least a costume from a film or television adaptation of an Austen novel, and was holding her hands behind her back. In them, she was clutching something dark, but I couldn't see what: a book maybe or a fan. Her long, dark, slightly wavy hair was coiled tidily at the nape of her neck, unlike my mother's rampant mane, but otherwise the resemblance to my mother was amazing.

My first thought, after the initial implosion of shock, was that my mother must have been to this very gallery; must have stood here, right where I was standing now, and been so impressed by the painting and its resemblance to her that she copied the pose when later photographed. At that moment, I felt close to her, which was an unusual, but welcome feeling for me. We were sharing the same space, the same view, the same thoughts, possibly even the same intake of breath on seeing the picture for the first time; it was only time that separated us and what was time? Then it occurred to me that whilst this take on events explained the shared pose in both images, it didn't explain the uncanny resemblance between the two women. What if Lily was a family member, my and my mother's ancestor? That would explain the shared looks, maybe even the similarity of pose; standing in a certain way might be a genetic disposition, mightn't it? There had to be something more. If Lily was family, albeit a long-dead ancestor rather than a living relative, at least it meant I had a family. It wasn't just Mother and me and the unknown, unlamented father. It wasn't just me alone. There were people out there to whom I was related. Moreover, if my relations were able to commission a painting of great, great, great Aunt Lily, it meant they had money. My ancestors were gentry. I came from wealthy, even noble stock.

The further thought that if they had once had money, some of my relations might still have some was just starting to nudge its way into my brain when I was found by my class teacher, berated for dragging my heels and wasting time, ushered out of the gallery, and put onto the coach back to school. Remonstrations that I needed to spend more time in front of the painting, and yet further time to find out about the background of the picture, went unheeded. I didn't even get a chance to buy a postcard of it. That was it. I had discovered my family and lost it again within the space of nine minutes. All I had were the stories seeded in my head: my mother at the gallery, standing in the exact spot I had stood and the long-lost wealthy relatives who one day would find out about me and would descend to sweep me up and away from the children's home and off to their grand mansion in the country. Those stories mattered. The first brought me closer to my mother. The second boosted my levels of hope and anticipation for several years, even if the hoped-for outcome was fated to remain firmly and disappointingly in the land of fiction. Both provided me with a sense of belonging, however vague, that I had not experienced before; a sense of being part of something beyond my own pathetic little borders. And if there was something bigger than me, and yet I was part of it, then that meant I existed all the more because of it.

* * *

So that was my childhood. As I said, it was unsettled, but not seriously, psychopathically unhappy. I made friends along the way, enemies too: lost them and made new ones. I learned to heal myself by telling stories, tapping into the power of words to illuminate, however poorly, the darkness that surrounded me. Eventually, I even forgave my mother for abandoning me - scars heal (or I learned to leave them in the dark places where I did not attempt to shine even the dimmest light).

My ability to stand back, observe and tell a good tale developed and eventually led me to take a course in journalism at my local college. This was followed, in time, by the offer of gainful, if ill-remunerated, employment with the local newspaper. I joined the world of wage packets and personal responsibility, and in so doing, I thought I had left my childhood behind.

IV

The sheer randomness of memory. A cascade of long, thick black hair, my hand snarled in its tendrils of patchouli and jasmine. A current of deep, dark water, a ribbon of heaving black satin, winding and coiling itself behind the streets of the city like the rolling waves of Van Gogh's starry skies up above the night. The feral noise of animals mating as the wilderness reinvades the town.

"I want you to come and take this child back now. Right now. He is an abomination. Be clear about this, I won't have him in this house a moment longer."
"Ssh, you'll wake him."
"I should care? I can't sleep with him here. Why should he?"
Had I woken up or was I still asleep? Am I asleep now? And if I'm still asleep, what will it take to wake me up for good?

"I want to be a writer."
"Fine, but how are you planning on earning a living?"
"I want to be a writer."
"Yes, I know you do, you've said already, but you'll need a trade to keep yourself, a proper job. Writing isn't a proper job at the best of times and certainly not for someone like you and anyway, what makes you think you can write well enough to get your work chosen?"
"Because I can. It's what I do."
"That's not what's written down here."
Looking. Just looking.

Two long, dark plaits hanging down over a summer gingham dress. White ankle socks against sun brown calves.

Then talking.

"*I can show you where the owls fly after dark.*"

"*Owls? There ain't no owls in town, silly.*"

"*Yes there are. I've heard them.*"

"*You're making it up. You don't get owls in London.*"

"*Yes you do. I've seen them, flying in the dark when the moon's not there.*"

"*'Ow can you see 'em if it's dark? You're either telling stories or you're barmy.*"

"*I'm not.*"

"*Are so too. Barmy army. Looney tunes.*"

"*It's true. I've seen them. I can show you.*"

"*Think you can get me in there with you? In the dark? You can think again, Mr. Looney Tunes. You're a mad bastard, you are.*"

One long dark plait lying all alone in a dustbin. Snip.

Long thick, black hair, curled around my fingers. Strands smelling of shampoo and tears, marking today in my diary for months. Snip.

Sometimes I wish the memories would just go away. Sometimes I think they're the only things I've got.

V

I may have chosen to leave my childhood behind, but it did not choose to leave me. It never let me get too far ahead, but caught up with me and continued to haunt me like a dark shape fluttering in the night. Incoherent mutterings and luminous owl eyes were relatively minor manifestations.

If truth be told, I don't think you can ever truly abandon your childhood. Yes, you can travel onward in time and into the demands and limitations of the waiting adult world, but your childhood is always there, too, alongside you the whole time, holding your hand. Like a child, it needs constant reassurance from the adult you. You are obliged to deal with its numerous anxieties and uncertainties. Your childhood never forgets, and, therefore, you must remember.

Looking at it dispassionately and scientifically, there is a resemblance between us and trees; each passing year gives us additional layers of experience and knowledge, adding to the original inner core, but not changing it. It remains as it was and cannot be extracted without irrevocably damaging the whole living edifice.

Whichever image you prefer, the effect is still the same: wherever you are, there is your childhood.

For all my proudly developed coping strategies, there are elements of my youth I would be more than happy to let go of, but they are part of me whether I want them to be or not. Conversely, there have been elements of my past I have wanted to hold onto and to understand better.

I tracked down the Black Moon Club in Soho, only to find it had long since closed and become a Chinese takeaway. I attempted to look up the rabbi who had found me and passed me on so rapidly, but he had been elderly then and had apparently passed on himself before I had even left school. I went back to the art gallery to rediscover that revelatory picture of Lily, but was surprised and upset to find there was no trace of it.

I have even attempted to get to know better the small child still resolutely clinging to my hand. Disregarding the feeble attempts by Social Services to unpack my head when I was young, I embarked on adult analysis, but with no breakthroughs, no revelations, and little sign of me. I didn't managed to reclaim any memories, false or otherwise, although one analyst swore blind he could find them (he didn't say if they would be the true or false variety) if I signed up for another twenty sessions and a corresponding overdraft for his fees. A therapist of a different persuasion said that just another five sessions, at a special higher rate given the circumstances, would enable her to catalogue the past lives she had stumbled over in previous sessions with me, but could offer me little assistance with my current one. A third, a Freudian, of course, thought that I might have a frustrated Oedipal complex, but as I walked out of his room at this point, I never did learn what he hoped to charge me to cure me of it.

I was obliged to seek my own salvation. Perhaps that goes to explain why I am writing these journal notes. If I can create something separate, but integral to me, both encompassing me and part of me, it makes my life that much more real. Describing something, telling a story about it, brings it further in to this world and embeds it in the here and now.

Over the years, I have described and reimagined the portrait of Lily as I saw her on that one and only occasion. This has made it all the more real for me, but hasn't enabled me to find her in the world of today.

I first went back to the gallery in search of Lily when I was sixteen. I stood on the spot both I and my mother had stood on before, but it was no longer just time separating us; this time there was no Lily to link us, just an eighteenth century bowl of fruit, a dead pheasant, and a couple of equally deceased hares. The warden for the room had only been working at the gallery for twelve months and had no knowledge of anything different having ever hung in that particular space.

I searched the rest of the eighteenth century rooms, but failed to find Lily. I started to search the rest of the really quite large gallery, but then realised it would be an impossible task in the time I had available. The girls on the information desk were as uninformative as their job descriptions required them to be. They assured me they had a still life with lilies and roses in the eighteenth century section of the catalogue, some water lilies straddling the nineteenth and twentieth centuries, a Lilith and serpent back in the nineteenth, and a copy of the gallery's full catalogue for sale at an extortionate price should I wish to conclude my investigations myself, which they would strongly encourage me to do as they had many other far more important things to be getting on with, thank you very much.

I failed to locate Lily on that occasion, but went back to the gallery a number of times after that, walked all the rooms, and eventually found the money to buy the catalogue. Lily remained lost.

The subsequent publication of images and art catalogues on the Internet and my ingrained terrier-like tendencies had me doing further research and raised my hopes again for a while, but I failed to find any trace of Lily in the gallery. She was most definitely no longer there, and there was no sign of her having been sold or lent to any other galleries. Via the Web, I broadened my search to other London galleries, then other U.K. galleries and eventually galleries and published images world wide. Lily remained as inscrutable as the Mona Lisa and less visible than the Virgin Mary. If she hadn't become so real to me with the passage of time and the many repetitions of her story, I might have begun to doubt I had ever seen her in the first place.

I held on to hope, but gave up on the act of searching until a further discovery brought the memory of Lily back with the impact of the trumpet section on the walls of fabled Jericho city.

VI

In addition to the usual tales of council tax increases, Machiavellian doings within the local Town Hall, and the occasional and highly lucrative "snake ate my cat" type stories that pay my rent and feed me, I harbour literary aspirations, or at least have developed a way of repotting the rampant shoots of narrative creation that regularly sprout within my head. I write short stories mostly, but also this journal, the odd appalling poem, and to date, one stubbornly unpublished novel. Yet, I persevere. I have all these stories within me and putting them down in solid black and white gives them the credibility they deserve. I have managed to get a reasonable number of short stories published, and I am convinced that if I build up a big enough body of externally published work that relates to me, is of me, but is so much bigger than me, then my place in the world will become stronger and clearer and will begin to make sense.

If I ever find Lily again, there will be another part of me that has been publicly evidenced and externally displayed. But the quest itself helps to justify me, just like the act of writing does: simultaneously physical and cerebral and with the benefit of it being deemed perfectly acceptable if the words shout at you through the silence. The latter relating more to writing than anything else, of course, but you know what I mean.

My quest has also had a number of subsidiary benefits. My visits to galleries and museums over the years have given me a collection of vivid images and painted narratives that have found their way into my stories and writing. The trips themselves have generated stories in their own right. Let me tell you one.

On this particular day, I was browsing through images in a gallery

I knew fairly well, if not intimately, looking for that unpredictable spark that would ignite another idea. I had no expectations of the visit, just hope. I wasn't even sure what sort of image I was looking for, just something of interest, a small shoot from which I could nurture a flourishing story. Nothing, however, was connecting, and I wandered vacantly into the basement area where both newly arrived and older, but unloved, acquisitions were stored higgledy piggledy in an indigestible mass. Maybe something would leap out at me from this heartburn inducing feast? And something did.

I didn't know whether to laugh, cry or throw up. There on a wall, between two lumpen still lifes, a poorly realised landscape of somewhere, and a health and safety notice, was Lily. Do I run towards her, walk forward nonchalantly, stand transfixed, or just scream? In practice, I think I did a bit of everything except the screaming. Somehow, and in some manner, I propelled my body forward to stand in front of her — except, and at that point I almost did throw up — it wasn't her. It had looked so like her: same face, same stance, same attitude, but this was a nineteenth century painting by a different hand from the one that had created Lily. If anything, it was better quality, a more painterly portrait; but it wasn't Lily. I had found her and lost her again within a bottomless forever of moments.

Why would a more skilled Victorian artist want to emulate an eighteenth century jobbing painter's piece? It wasn't a straight copy; the clothes the woman was wearing were different from Lily's, the background was different, vaguer, but the face was still Lily's, and therefore, as far as I was concerned, although it wasn't Lily, it was still my mother.

For once the gallery was helpful.

"Slow down, love. Deep breaths. Now tell me again what flowers you're after?"

The woman at the desk pieced together my incoherent ramblings and produced, not only the details of the artist and the portrait, but also a postcard of this new found image that I could take away as proof of what I had seen. This time I had evidence.

"It's the Striga painting, but it's bright red flowers, not lilies, on her dress. See?"

Lily, it appeared, had been transformed into Mrs. Striga, a nineteenth century society hostess. Still the same three-quarter pose towards the observer, head held high; still the same direct, challenging stare; still the hands clasping something behind the back. But this time, the dress was black, low-cut and embroidered with blood red flowers that matched the large red flowers pinned to her bodice. The background to the painting was plain: a mottled green/brown with what could almost be a willow leaf pattern hiding in its depths. Her lightly waved hair was still pulled back to the nape of her neck, but in the fashion of the later century; not like Lily's. The sitter looked to be roughly the same age as I remembered Lily being, late twenties or early thirties, but as this portrait had been painted over seventy years after Lily's image was captured in paint, I had to accept Mrs. Striga could not be Lily.

I was confused. Two paintings of almost identical women in identical poses painted over seventy years apart — why? Had the Victorian artist, who was reasonably well known in the salons of the period, cut a few creative corners and copied Lily rather than create afresh?

"Sorry, love, You'll have to look into that yourself."

My subsequent research highlighted that a Mrs. Striga had actually existed and would have been as well known as the painter, if not better, in the salons of the capital. A copy of someone else's portrait, however flattering, was not going to be successfully passed off as that of a well-known socialite. Was it, therefore, intended as a joke or an homage? I wondered if I had remembered the details of Lily's painting correctly. Were the two paintings really so alike? The image of Lily was so clear in my head with its midnight blue Jane Austen dress that I could not accept I had remembered it wrongly. And what of my mother's photograph? That was real enough. A third, almost identical, image captured on film ninety years after the Striga painting. Even if I had remembered Lily wrongly, I still had the photograph. Which of the two paintings had my mother seen? Perhaps, like me, she had seen both, and that was why she was so taken with the pose. Sure, she would have had to have been very conscious of the detail of the pose to replicate it so well, but who wouldn't be when confronted with two such striking mirror images of yourself. The coincidence of all three women looking so alike would have ensured it was well and truly embedded in her memory. But that in itself raised yet another question: just why did these women look so alike?

The only logical explanation I could come up with, and I had managed to come up with an amazing number of really far-fetched ones, was heredity. They had to be family: my family. I had friends and work colleagues who were always carping on about how much their amorphous, all-babies-actually-look-alike progeny were the spitting image of them or their partners or even some other invariably distant family member. I could never see it, but perhaps they were right. I had never heard of such really close physical similarity across generations before, but then, look at the English Royal Family. Noses, ears, chins: Notwithstanding the odd outcropping of ginger, you can tell who's in the firm by blood and who isn't. If the House of Windsor can have a pretty good go at breeding blue blood clones, why shouldn't my family go one better? I no longer had any doubt: Lily, Mrs. Striga, and my mother were all related and, most importantly, were all related to *me*. They were my family, my links to the past, my roots. And those roots nourished my present. Because of them, my life was both bigger and smaller at the same time. But most importantly, it had taken a firmer foothold in the here and now.

With the discovery of Mrs. Striga, I now had a name and a background that I could research. My mother had only left a photograph. Lily was just a once-seen image and a single name. Mrs. Striga, however, was a fixed fact in history. She had a surname, a marital status, and a documented position in London society. I was sure I could track her down.

I became a man on a mission.

In some ways, it proved easier than I expected. The portrait artist was better known than I had realised, and his works were meticulously documented and catalogued. The painting was apparently one of the last he produced. Mrs. Striga had been painted in 1879 at the request of an admirer of the sitter herself and had been purchased by him upon its completion. It had subsequently been donated anonymously to the gallery in 1946.

I checked the London newspaper archives for 1879 and sure enough, in the society pages, there were references to Mrs. Striga. Working backwards, I found references to her as far back as 1876 and moving forward, up to 1890, but nothing beyond then.

The articles I found related to events and attendances at social gatherings. They described where Mrs. Striga had been, who she had been with, and sometimes, what she was wearing when she went there. There was never any mention of her age; the society press back then were circumspect and not age-obsessed as they are now. Nor was there mention of her marriage or, indeed, a Mr. Striga. Researching forward from 1890 within a likely time period, then a less likely one, and finally throughout every year from then to 1970, I could find no reference to her death. I did discover that around 1880 she had occupied a large townhouse close to Regents Park and London Zoo. From there, I tracked her down to the national census for 1881 and struck lucky when I found a Mrs. L. Striga living at an appropriate address. Inconveniently, no age was given. There was no mention of a Mr. Striga living at the house, so it was possible that Mrs. Striga was a wealthy widow. There was no reference for her at the same address for either the 1871 or 1891 censuses, so there the trail stopped. I could guess at her age from the 1879 painting, but without details of her marriage or her maiden name, I had little more to work on. At least, however, I now knew more about her than Lily, or even my own mother. It was like lighting intermittent candles on the long slow journey down into the dark basement of my life.

VII

I must admit that for extended periods of my adult life there has been nothing much worth writing about, if you are looking for the stuff of event-fuelled biography. I haven't done much or gone anywhere of note. I have always remained in London. Some would say, and indeed have done, that I am unduly inert, that I've never had the initiative to move on and out. Maybe that's true, but I've had my reasons for staying put. London is such a beautiful city, and it's my home. It's the city where I was found, and I grew up here. It contains my memories in just the same way a beer glass holds a pint of smoothly liquid amber London Pride. I know its sounds, its smells, its pictures. I can sense its histories, its multifaceted past. Each time I walk down the street, catch a bus, hop on the tube, I gulp down those memories all over again. There's much to be said for a decent pint of bitter when you're parched and gasping for a drink. London's my favourite pint.

If my mother ever thinks of me at all, her memories, however peripheral, will bind me to North London and the place where she abandoned me to the flow of fate. If she ever wants to look for me, that's where she'll have to start. North of the Thames has therefore retained an aura of tantalising possibility for me. Whenever I've been tempted to roam, it has whispered my name, and I've always come running back: expectant, loyal and patiently waiting.

My work is based in London. I quite like my job. I have a reasonable place to live, and I love the anonymity of living in a big city. Millions of people constantly stirred together in this mixing bowl of time and place, and yet you can squat like the lush cherry on top of the trifle, never having to interact except at the most superficial of levels unless you want to. Alternatively, if you crave human contact, there are millions of people to choose from, and you can keep picking and choosing indefinitely.

I love the buzz, the energy that London gives off as all those souls go about their business, whatever it is. Just stand on Waterloo Bridge around sunset and watch as a river of as-yet-untold stories flows and rushes past you. As the sun goes down, just look at how the city's lights glitter and spark off the liquid river at your feet. It's an electric charge of energy and anticipation, like a jolt from the live wire of life. Re-energized, you can make your way home to shut your front door and insulate yourself from the otherwise draining demands of modern day-to-day living.

Abandoned in my baby basket, like an offering to the absent God of the synagogue, I was better wrapped in London than I ever was in my none-too-warm blankets, and London has never stopped swaddling me. To this day, I wrap myself in it like an old, well-sucked security blanket. It has never abandoned me. How could I ever abandon it? So, if at times my life has been uninspiring, there has always been more than adequate compensation in the surrounding excitement and inspiration of the Metropolis. It has never let me down in the way that people have. I dare say that some of my former girlfriends may take exception to this point of view. There have been at least three of them who saw themselves as both inspirational and central to my existence, but somehow my existence never seemed to catch on to this. Does that sound callous? I don't mean it to, but as lovely and luscious as those ladies most certainly were, as much as I was fond of them in my own slightly disconnected way, I never loved any of them enough to choose them for life. I guess if I am honest, I never really loved any of them. But then again, what has love got to do with it?

I suppose that's callous, but at least it's honest. Surely it's better to be honest and own up when the connection is not strong enough, than lie and pretend to be in love and end up going through the motions for life? Mind you, Angela did not think so.

Angela Ormond: blonde, blue-eyed, a Botticelli angel, an exceedingly sexy Botticelli angel, with whom I lived for three years.

"Abe, you should try harder. If you just tried a bit harder, a bit more often, then things would sort themselves out. You need to get off your backside and do stuff, even if you don't believe in it. Doing stuff makes other stuff happen, better stuff. Don't think of it as going through the motions. If you do it enough times, it becomes real."

I am not sure what specifically this piece of advice related to, but I don't think it really matters. Angela's advice was invariably the same regardless of the issue in question: my job, my writing, our life together, sexual dysfunction, world peace. Angela believed in positive thinking and positive action.

"You need to be more positive, Abe. You are too...inert. Think positive and things become positive. There's no benefit in mooning around the house all day looking at bloody paintings on that bloody computer of yours. You'll end up back in hospital. Get out there and do something."

Or the classic, "It's only a cat; go out and get another one." That last piece of exquisite sensitivity being delivered less than twenty four hours after Lily, my much-loved cat, was run over in the street. I guess Angela and I were never going to make it, but I did sort of understand where she was trying to come from in terms of doing things enough times to make them real.

Now Lucy was totally different from Angela in the way that night is totally different from the day that precedes it. Lucy was dark: long dark hair, hazel eyes. Petite but wonderfully curvaceous, sensitive, sympathetic, sensuous, and hot: in bed, on the floor, on the kitchen table — you get the picture. Lucy and I should have worked out, but somehow we didn't. I wanted sex; she wanted sex and its aftermath — children. In the end, she left me for an accountant and within seven months they had started a family. I guess she had started doing the books with him before she finally closed her account with me.

Please don't think this is just a feeble excuse for me to run through my back catalogue of leading ladies. This is about me, or the story I want to tell of me. You should therefore know about Jenny.

Jenny was different, except that, physically speaking she was actually a lot like Lucy: taller, older, but equally curvy and with long dark hair, dark grey eyes and a sensitive soul. If anything, she turned out to be a bit too sensitive, but that came later.

Jenny and I met at an art gallery. For me it was lust at first sight. From her point of view I wasn't bad looking, had (on closer enquiry) the right star sign (almost certainly Gemini) and produced an initially promising, if slightly unusual, tarot reading. We started going out together regularly, then stayed in together regularly and then, in time honoured fashion, moved in together.

Jenny helped me in my never ending search for the painting of Lily and, in due course, assisted me with my research on Mrs. Striga. For a while, she became concerned I was becoming rather obsessive, but as the research ground to a halt, things settled down and our relationship started to move forward. Then the dreams started.

First it was me. The old nightmares came back and I began to hear whispering voices as soon as I started waking up or, alternatively, I would wake up suddenly and with a start, feeling as if I was falling. Some nights, I would imagine things fluttering around the bedroom and, of course, those large and luminous eye globes of my infancy returned to haunt me. I would wake myself up with my dreams and, more often than not, wake Jenny, too. She put up with the interrupted sleep for a while, but then came to the conclusion that a serious tarot reading was called for in order to identify my problem and address it. She had read for me before, so it wasn't too big a deal, but this time things didn't go as she expected. For starters, she really didn't like the cards I had drawn.

"They're nearly all major arcana. That's really odd. I don't like that. Normally there are more court or pip cards. No Abs, stop that. What are you doing? Please don't do that. Oh Abs, you really shouldn't have done that."

I had picked up the seven cards I had just selected, reshuffled them and dealt them in a horseshoe shape as I had sometimes seen Jenny do. The first card I had laid down was the Moon, a card I was particularly drawn to, as in Jenny's tarot pack the picture of the moon was accompanied by an image of a saucer eyed owl. The next card was the Priestess and then the Lovers, the three of swords, the two of swords, Death and the World.

"Look," I tried to reassure her, "there are two number cards, a two and a three from the same suit. They're not all major arcane thingies, although this whole thing is pretty arcane, if you ask me." Jenny burst into tears and ran out of the room. Another case of my inappropriate humour. Her upset upset me. I swept the cards off the table with my arm before running after her. I managed to convince her that it wasn't the end of the world, and after much crying and hugging, she calmed down, but still wouldn't say what the matter was, other that it was a bad hand and my flippancy had upset her.

She was clearly still edgy when we walked back into the room enroute to the kitchen and the soothing panacea of making a pot of tea together. The cards were lying on the floor where I had flung them. They had landed in a rough half circle in what, surprisingly, looked like the order I had dealt them. Jenny took a sharp intake of breath when she saw them.

"Oh Abs," she said and dissolved into tears again. Eventually, I quietened her down enough for her to explain, at least superficially, the problem. "They're the same way as before. That's more than coincidence. It's like the cards are shouting. It's not good. I can't, I won't, give you a reading on that," she said, pointing to the cards on the floor as if they were a dollop of cat shit. "Don't ask me to give you a reading."

I, of course, did. She resisted at first, but I am very good at doing pathetic and pleading and eventually she gave in. "Okay, I'll tell you about the individual cards in isolation, text book stuff, but that's all I'll do. Okay?" I naturally concurred. What else could I have done?

"The Moon is a very negative card. It's in your past, so at least we can be grateful about that, but it speaks of despair and depression, loneliness, and a tangled web of negativity." Fair dos. That didn't sound too cheerful, but it was text book and in the past, and any resonance with what she was saying was just the fading echo of chaos passing.

"The High Priestess is to do with intuition and your feminine side, but upside down, it says more about suppression or hidden issues, something lacking or missing. The Lovers card shows Adam and Eve. It talks about choosing, making tough decisions, honouring commitments. Three of Swords is bad. It symbolises serious pain,

sorrow and suffering, total confusion: mental, spiritual, the lot."
Now, even I had to admit that didn't sound so good.

"The Two of Swords isn't much better. Like the Lovers, it
symbolises duality, but in this case, things are balancing on a sword
edge, different possibilities open to you. Courage is there, but also
violence and treachery. The seventh card, the World, is normally
a good card. When it is the right way up, it signifies wholeness,
completeness, the successful completion of something. Upside
down it can mean frustration, or an inability to complete something
satisfactorily."

"And in my case?"

"I can't say. A reading is holistic. It considers all the cards together
and their relationships to one another and to you. I was only going
to tell you about the individual cards. Also, I don't really know. It's
because it fell sideways so it's neither one thing nor another"

"And what about the Death card?"

"Sorry?"

"What about Death, the sixth card that you skirted over? It is
Death, isn't it?"

Jenny paused long enough for me to know that she was probably
about to lie. I had always been better at story telling than she was.

"Not necessarily. Not automatically, but yes sometimes it can be,
but then again, sometimes it can mean different things. When it's
the right way up, it can mean change, the beginning of something
new and good."

"But when it's upside down like this one?"

Jenny seemed to be getting tearful again. "It's not a good sign, but
it can still just mean change, bad rather than good change, or slow,
painful change or…"

"So overall, not a good hand, then?" I have always considered
understatement to be a much underrated expression of wit, a sign of
ironic intellectual disengagement, but it just reduced Jenny to more
tears, so I took it as a no and gave up.

We went to bed early that night. It seemed like a good idea to put
a bad day behind us. This time, however, it was Jenny's turn to have

nightmares. Twice she woke up screaming or crying, but each time she refused to tell me why.

The next day, neither of us was at our best. We soldiered on through the day, but lack of sleep was showing, and we both decided that another attempt at an early night was in order. It appeared, however, that the season of all natures was still denied us.

As soon as I fell asleep I was falling, faster and faster, not into the ubiquitous owl eyes, but into the dark, open beak of a huge bird. I woke up with a start, and though I sank back to oblivion almost immediately, Jenny said that I started muttering in my sleep and kept it up for the whole time she remained awake, which was, I am told, well into the dark of the night. Eventually, she fell asleep, too, only to find herself in the middle of a barren red desert, lost, alone and surrounded by hissing snakes. And so it went on, but not just for that one night. Night after night, both of us suffered vivid nightmares, assuming we were able to get to sleep in the first place.

Jenny was becoming more and more strung out and consulted a healer she knew. She came back bearing two dream catchers, four amulets, and an armful of scented candles. I couldn't sleep with the candles lit because of the light and a half-admitted fear that we would end up burning the house down. The dream catchers didn't seem to have any effect whatsoever, but the amulets did seem to do something, and we both started sleeping better for the next month or so. Then my nightmares came back. Mostly I was falling, but sometimes things were out there, trying to break in through the bedroom window. If I was lucky, they remained nameless, fluttering shadows. At other times, they were owls, or the sinuous branches of a huge willow tree, or a flying yellow-eyed snake with huge smoky black wings. None of it was good, and if it now seems rather fanciful in the reassuring light of day, it didn't seem that way in the dark of another unquiet night. Jenny said that I was now muttering regularly in my sleep and keeping her awake. I think she had started having nightmares again, too, but wouldn't admit it.

Jenny went back to her healer, replenished the amulets, and things improved for another month. Then it started up all over again. Jenny consulted horoscopes and moon charts and, having determined that it was an entirely lunar issue, seemed almost disappointed that the relapses didn't coincide with the full moon. She was a great believer in the primal power of the lunar cycle and the impact of moon tides, and propounded, with an almost religious fervour, that the full moon had the strongest mystical effect of all the moon's phases. So much for religion. If anything, the nightmares seemed to coincide with the waning of the moon. Anyway, Jenny went back to her healer, and we endured. There wasn't much else we could do.

Then Jenny started getting up in the night and sleep walking. Once I came round to find her trying to ride me, which was pretty okay as far as I was concerned, but seemed surprisingly to distress her. Other times, less erotically, she rearranged the furniture in either the bedroom or the lounge. How I managed to sleep through this, I don't know. It was either the sleep of the virtuous or the sleep of the dead, but either way, the outcome was the same. I would go to bed in an ordered and tidy house and would wake up to find the dining chairs in the bedroom or the bedroom rug on the dining table, or any one of a number of inter-room furniture arrangements. Jenny denied all responsibility for the nocturnal interior re-design and blamed me. But, as I knew it wasn't me, it had to be her. We rowed about it, but nothing ever got resolved.

What with the restless nights and the frequent furniture re-arranging, we were both pretty tired and stressed, and the rows became worse. A temper I didn't know I had clawed its way up to the surface. At times, things became unpleasant. We also lost the solace of good hard sex after a bad row to make things better. I was too tired to get or keep things up and Jenny had a permanent headache from too little sleep. Things went from bad to worse.

I think the lack of sex became the final straw. We were both frustrated and feverishly pent up. I started dreaming about it — sex, that is. Graphic, sweating, heaving copulation. My restless nights were now disturbed by sweaty, but divinely fleshy visitations. In my sleep, beautiful women would turn up with just one overriding desire: to fuck me. Hell, those dreams were luridly good, but they didn't give me any respite. I woke up more horny than ever. Until, that is, the dreams became so good, and I became so wound up, that I came in my sleep.

The first time Jenny was amused, and I was slightly embarrassed. It brought back unwanted memories of adolescence. The second time was a drag because we had to change the sheets again. Yet, as time progressed, I began to enjoy myself more and more, and Jenny became less and less happy. Sticky sheets were a mild irritant. More worryingly, she started to feel superfluous to my increasingly active, if somnambulistic and onanistic, sex life. Our relationship accelerated downhill.

During the day, we were both at work, and when I was at home, I was half asleep most of the time, too tired to discuss things, too drained to do anything much, let alone make love to Jenny. Come night time, I apparently came across as insensitively eager to go to bed, quick to fall asleep, and generally too wrapped up in my sweat-drenched fantasy love life to pay attention to the needs of a flesh and blood partner I almost appeared to have forgotten. One morning, as she had to wipe off the proof of my nightly satisfaction yet again, she told me that I had started to sicken her. It was not long after that she left me for the healer. I was once more back on my own. At which point, the dreams came to an abrupt and unexpected halt.

VIII

I am happy enough in my own company. There are always plenty of nameless stories to listen to in any bar or café in this city should I be overcome by an unexpected need for human contact, but I did miss Jenny and, equally, I missed the soiled excitement of the dreams. For a while there, I admit, I wanted to hurt Jenny, to punish her and get my own back for her walking out on me, but the feeling didn't last for too long. I rationalised her departure as just another in a lifetime's list of going aways. My temper waned. The anger cooled and walked out on me, too. Life had turned back to the uneventful and the mundane, but this time, life's routines didn't feel as comforting or as complete as before. Even London felt empty, as if something was absent from it. Its urban pleasures had become surprisingly flaccid.

In a way, I still feel that something has excused itself from my life and that is why finding Eve has been so wonderful. It has been like waking up or, conversely, like returning to a half-remembered, but vividly familiar dream. In either event, I now have another story to tell.

It was at the gallery where I had come across the Mrs. Striga painting. I had been invited to a drinks do for The Friends of the Gallery — part fund raising, part P.R., that type of thing — and had decided to go along for the free booze, a chance to look at the paintings, and on the off chance that I could work up a story for the paper. To that end, I was dutifully schmoozing the gallery's marketing assistant when she suggested I ought to meet some of the patrons. She lead me across the reception area to a group of obviously wealthy, rather elderly, and probably very boring old farts who were deep in conversation regarding their collective share performance. The one exception to this unpromising gaggle of the great and the good had her back to me. But, from what I could see of her beyond the curtain of long black hair hanging down to her waist, she was neither old, nor promised to be boring.

"Eve, may I introduce you to Abe Finchley from our local paper. Abe, this is Eve Striga, one of our most generous patrons."

The woman with the long black hair turned round, and I almost dropped my wine glass. There, directly in front of me, was the spitting image of the painted Mrs. Striga and of Lily, and of my mother.

Eve Striga politely and gamefully unwound the silence that had so obviously wrapped itself around us following my extremely audible intake of breath.

"Abe, how nice to meet you. What brings you to our august gathering of art lovers and their wallets?" As she was speaking, she had taken my arm and walked the pair of us away from the marketing assistant and the group of elderly shareholders. "Whatever your motivation for being here, I am very glad that you have turned up to rescue me from the antiquities section." She smiled.

By this time, I had managed to start breathing again and had gathered up sufficient of my remaining intellectual faculties to gabble something about journalistic duties and support for the gallery. Whilst I was attempting to organise some more words, at least partially coherently, we had carried on walking and the next thing I was painfully aware of was the pair of us standing in front of the Mrs. Striga portrait. The resemblance between Eve Striga and her namesake was stronger than my memory had believed or accepted. My jaw metaphorically and literally dropped, and whatever words I had been preparing scarpered back down my throat without any concern for the order of their going.

"You've noticed the similarity then?" she said dryly and moved forward in order to stand directly in front of the portrait in the exact same pose that had been etched into my consciousness since my consciousness had begun. I maintained my silence; it was the least I could do given the circumstances. It was all I could do, if I was honest.

"She is my great, great, great aunt, give or take a great or two in either direction," said Eve. "You just can't beat the genes."

My brain began to regain a sense of feeling as the blood cautiously returned to my head. I could feel my thoughts starting to run around like ants in very heavy hobnail boots. *Is she family? Do I tell her about my research into Mrs. Striga, or about Lily, or my mother? Does she know my mother? Have I found a relative? Can I really tell her any of this? I'm going to come across as obsessed or mad or both.*

"You look like you've seen a ghost?"

My tongue reclaimed some semblance of poise before the rest of me did, "Quite possibly, but if I have, then it's a very lovely and charming ghost."

She smiled again. "As I said, you can't beat the genes."

I decided to tell her something of my fascination with her great, great, great aunt and the possible tie-in to my imagined family, whilst toning it down a little so she didn't think I was obsessed, Oedipal, crazy, or just plain needy. She listened encouragingly and without making any obvious attempts to run away or cry out for help. I like to think my references to the attractiveness of the family genes may have helped.

"I don't think I've ever come across the painting of Lily, but it wouldn't surprise me if she was family, too. The family resemblance down through the generations is quite striking." This was said as her dark brown eyes fixed my dark brown ones with an appraising, but not unfriendly, stare. "A lot of stuff has been passed down through the generations. Do you have the photograph of your mother with you?"

"No. It's safe. I mean, I like to keep it safe. It's the only thing I have of her, you see, so I like to keep it safe. I keep it at home so that I can keep it safe." I ground to an embarrassed halt. I was becoming verbally incontinent and with the vocabulary of a five-year-old to add to my shambling discomfort.

"Tell you what," she said, handing over an expensively plain business card, "Give me a call tomorrow, and we can arrange to meet up for a drink or dinner and you can show me the photograph of your mother. Maybe we can start to work out the connections." She moved away towards the exit making the phone gesture with her left hand. "Call me. I mean it. Do call me." And with that, she was gone.

Several stiff drinks later and I was pumping the marketing assistant for all she knew about Eve Striga, but it wasn't much more than I already knew: probably early thirties, related to the Mrs. Striga in the portrait, living in London, had contacted the gallery eighteen months or so ago, because of the family connection to the painting to see if she could help out in some way, and had been extremely generous in supporting the gallery ever since. The marketing assistant couldn't recall what exactly she had donated to the gallery, but by then she had had at least as many stiff drinks as me, so the memory lapse was hardly surprising.

I decided it was my turn to exit into the homeward flow of the London night, on the grounds that the sooner I got home, the sooner I could go to bed, and the sooner tomorrow could be here. It wasn't just my vocabulary that wanted to relive being five. It was like Christmas and childhood had come all over again.

IX

The next morning was spent trying to work out how soon I could phone Eve Striga without seeming too eager. Her business card only displayed a name and a phone number. It was not giving anything away. Surprisingly, the name was L. Striga, not E. Striga, and I hoped this didn't mean there was a Mr. L. Striga lurking in the wings. Whilst my main motivation for phoning Eve was, I assured myself, to do with my search for my mother and my roots, I was willing to admit that I was very taken with Eve herself. Long, thick dark hair, big dark eyes, all parts in the right place and in the very right proportion, reasonably young, but not that much younger than me: what was not to like?

By midday I decided that I had left it long enough and therefore phoned her. It was funny, I was nervous like an adolescent on a first date, except it had been a long time since I had been an adolescent, and back in those days I hadn't been nervous. I was scared she might be out. I was scared she might be in. I was scared she wouldn't want to meet up, after all. I hadn't realised it was possible to be so many kinds of scared in so short a period of time. Fortunately for me, she answered the phone after just two rings and seemed genuinely pleased to hear from me.

Yes, she did still want to meet up. Soon would be good. What was I doing now and how long would it take me to get up to town? That was great. Did I want to meet her for a late lunch? She'd meet me at Seven Dials at two. There was a little restaurant nearby that she rated. Did I want to take down her mobile number in case of accidents? And that was that. So, just why was my heart beating so fast?

In the end, I got up to Covent Garden slightly ahead of schedule and rang her mobile. She gave me directions to the restaurant near Trinity Passage, and I made my own way there. It turned out that I didn't really need detailed directions, as the restaurant was very close to where the Black Moon Club had been and where the Chinese takeaway that had replaced it was still, presumably, located. Strangely enough, I couldn't see the takeaway, though, from recollection, it had to be very close, if not actually adjacent to La Luna, Eve's restaurant of choice. Then again, my memory on the matter had grown hazy.

Eve was already sitting down at a table when I arrived. She stood up to give me a brief, almost maternal, kiss on the cheek and then promptly sat down again, indicating that I should do the same. Suddenly, everything seemed horribly formal. I wasn't sure what to say, and the words were once again bottle-necking in my throat. I was grateful when she suggested we concentrate on the menu so that we could order reasonably quickly. Studying the entrees gave me a chance to get my words under control and regain command of myself sufficiently to at least give the appearance of being a mature adult.

Dishes selected and our order placed with an attentive waiter, Eve asked to see the photograph of my mother. There was a brief silence as she studied the picture.

"She could be me," was all she said.

"Exactly. Now you can see why meeting you is such a big thing for me."

"Is it now?" she replied. "Is it really a big thing for you?"

There was a further silence. I didn't know how to respond. I breathed in hard and waited. At which point, I was saved from yet more embarrassment by the arrival of our bottle of wine. It was the special house red. Eve had recommended it. I have no idea what it was actually called, but it was strikingly dark in colour, almost black. At least its unusual shade gave me a topic of conversation, and as we drank more and more of the bottle, I found my tongue loosening commensurately.

We talked about everything and anything. We talked so much that I can't remember the half of it, but I can still recall the crucial, if remarkably brief, bits about her family and Eve herself.

"My family history goes back a long way chronologically and has travelled quite a distance geographically, too. The roots were originally in the Middle East, the hair and eye colouring give it away, but that was a very long time ago. I am sure that by Mrs. Striga's day, any non-European links would have been firmly forgotten in public and absolutely unmentionable. God forbid.

"As I said last night, the Mrs. Striga of the gallery painting was my great, to the power of several, aunt. Knowing about the painting, I decided to follow through on the family connections and offer my services to the gallery, for what they are worth. The gallery graciously accepted them, and here we are.

"I really don't know anything about the Lily painting you say you've seen, but given the resemblance you describe and the strength of the family genes across the generations, she may well be another ancestor. It's a shame you don't have any more details about her or her portrait or we could look into things in more detail.

"Your mother, if this is indeed her," (now why did she have to go and say that?), "looks like one of the family, but I'm afraid I can't place her. I guess she would be old enough to be my mother, too, but I can tell you she's not. I don't know, though, who she could be. Do you know anything about her?"

I repeated and expanded upon the story of my abandonment and discovery in the wilds of darkest Finchley and the lack of information I actually had about my mother. Eve appeared intrigued by the fact that the Black Moon Club had been so close to where we now were, but seemed unsurprised that I could no longer locate the site of the club and had been unable to recognise its former premises on the way over to the restaurant.

"Memory fades with the passing of time. It's both inevitable and desirable, don't you think? Remembering absolutely everything would be intolerable. It'd be enough to drive you mad."

She also, rather pointedly I felt, commented yet again that there was no guarantee that the woman in the photograph was actually my mother. Although she then tempered her remarks by adding that I did appear to have the family looks. I wondered whether this repeated distancing of me from her family had anything to do with the apparent family wealth, but as she skilfully skirted round any attempts I made to raise the subject of family inheritance, I couldn't be sure. I didn't feel, at this very early stage in our relationship, it would be particularly desirable to grab the bull by the horns and ask outright if she or her relatives were still loaded.

As for her own personal circumstances, the most important thing I learned that afternoon was that there wasn't a Mr. Striga. The L on the business card was her. The initial was for her actual first name,

"But, I don't like it very much and rarely use it; it's so old fashioned. I much prefer Eve. It's short, timeless, and elegant and, additionally, my using it pissed off my ex-husband deliciously, so I used it all the more and it kind of stuck."

I wanted to know more about the ex-husband, but somehow the discussion wandered off the subject and a sense of old fashioned politeness stopped me from pursuing the point against the flow of the conversation. Eve was, by now, telling me she'd been out of the country for some time and had come back to Britain just over eighteen months ago. She was keen to re-establish old connections and make new ones, hence her approach to the gallery. When I asked what contact she had with her family here, she simply repeated that she had been out of the country for a while and was re-establishing connections. She had come back to the house at Regents Park, and yes it was the house that Mrs. Striga had once lived in, and was now in the process of getting her local affairs back in order.

The conversation then went off on another tangent as we continued to talk about everything and anything, but not much more about the family or my possible connections to it. Eve was an elegant and effortless conversationalist: intelligent, entertaining, enthralling, and drop dead gorgeous. I was captivated, and I admit my focus was now solely on enjoying the moment. Subconsciously, I was aware there were things I wanted to discuss that never seemed to float to the surface of the conversation, but it didn't seem to matter that much. Right at the end of the meal as Eve was resolving things with the waiter, I did take the opportunity to raise the question of religion. Perhaps I should have offered to pay, rather than come over all theological, but Eve seemed to be in control of the evening. I, sure as hell, wasn't.

"One of the things I've always wondered about was religion, well at least my religion. Being abandoned on the steps of a synagogue did raise a few questions. You mentioned that the Strigas were originally from the Middle East. Does that mean that they, I mean, that *we* are Jewish?"

Did I see a flare of anger in her eyes when I asked that question? If I did, she didn't let it show overtly in her, admittedly somewhat dismissive, response.

"Well now, we still really can't say about you, can we? Yes, you have an Old Testament name, but what's in a name? You can't prove who your mother is, let alone who you are, which does rather leave you in limbo, so to speak. For me, personally, I think the whole God thing is rather overrated and is far more bother than it's worth. I prefer to have as little to do with organised, patriarchal religion as possible. It's been said, you know, that 'An honest God is the noblest work of man,' but I have never found mankind to be that noble." And with that, the conversation was closed.

Looking back now, there were a remarkable number of loose ends just left dangling. I may not be of the journalistic calibre of a reporter from the nationals, but I am surprised that I let so many things just float away from me. In my defence, this wasn't work, and I didn't want to spoil the good time I was having just being with Eve. Nevertheless, this was my big opportunity to find out about what I believed to be my family, and I didn't take it. I just accepted the crumbs that Eve tossed my way and hardly questioned anything she told me. I guess my growing infatuation with her meant I was keener to look forward than be reflective or use up precious time peering backwards. The big question for me was when was I going to see her next? Fortunately, it didn't look as if I would have long to wait. As we left the restaurant she asked for my phone number and promised to call me within the next couple of days.

X

I was on tenterhooks all the next day, a Tuesday, hoping that Eve would phone and practising what I would say to her when she did. I was eager to see her again. The possible family connection was the culmination of half a lifetime's anticipation, but Eve herself was more exciting still.

When she didn't phone on Tuesday, I was disappointed, like a child who is told they cannot have their Christmas presents until Boxing Day. When she didn't phone on Wednesday's Boxing Day, I became depressed. Fortunately for me, Christmas finally came on the day after Boxing Day.

The phone rang.

"Hi Abe, it's Eve. Do you fancy meeting up for dinner tomorrow night?"

What was there to say but yes? Other commitments could, and did, go out the window.

"I'd love to. When, where, and this time it's my shout, okay?"

"Eight o'clock tomorrow would be good for me. Would you mind eating at La Luna again? It's very convenient. Trouble is, though, you won't be able to pay for dinner."

"Eight o'clock is fine. La Luna is fine, but why can't I buy you dinner?"

"Oh, it's all a bit embarrassing really. I actually own La Luna, so I couldn't possibly have you pay."

Well, that certainly put me in my place and at the same time highlighted that Eve, at least, was not without assets, whilst yours truly was little more than a charity case, the impoverished probably distant cousin. Still, I wanted to see Eve again, so what price pride?

* * *

Eve was already at La Luna when I got there. She looked beautiful. Although the restaurant was dark and lit primarily by the candles on the tables, Eve seemed almost luminous. I couldn't tell you what she was wearing, but whatever it was appeared to shimmer.

This time her greeting kiss was somewhat less maternal. That was fine by me.

She smiled. "I'm so pleased you could make it tonight. Knowing I'd phoned at the last minute, I was afraid you might have other commitments."

"Absolutely not," I lied. The relationship in question was on the way out, so what was a cancelled date, here or there?

"Let's order some wine. The house special is always good."

"Well, you would know." I hadn't meant to be cranky, but I admit I had been taken aback by what I felt was the belated discovery that La Luna was her restaurant, and I obviously was not yet over it. It came out somewhat unexpectedly in my voice.

Eve seemed surprised too. "Abe, I am sorry. We can always go somewhere else if you'd rather."

I thought about it. "No, I'm good with the restaurant. I was just surprised to find that you owned it, but hadn't thought to mention the fact before."

"Does it matter?"

Thinking about it logically for a second, it didn't really matter, but I had been embarrassed by the discovery. It had made me feel like a cross between a pauper cousin in need of a hand out and a sulky five-year-old whose best friend hadn't let him in on a secret. Eve seemed to be reading my mind, or perhaps it was just my face.

"Sorry, it does matter. I must have made you feel like an impecunious country cousin receiving unwanted largesse from your gentrified relatives. It was also a bit like me keeping a secret from you when there was no need to."

"Uh huh. It did rather feel like that."

"Sorry. I really do mean sorry. I didn't consciously set out to keep things hidden, but the opportunity to tell you never seemed to crop up, and it seemed rather patronising just to drop it into the conversation. Also, and okay, I'll admit it now, the evening in the gallery, when we first met up, I did wonder if you were pursuing me with a tale of possible family connections because of the money. Now I've spent time with you and have seen the photograph of,"— did I detect a slight pause? — "your mother, I know this isn't the case and that you are genuine."

I was partially placated. At least she had seemed to understand why I was cranky and had said sorry. Her admitted lack of trust grated a little, but I now knew my childhood daydream of long lost wealthy relatives was rooted in some fact. Eve clearly had money, and it seemed likely that collectively, the family was not without. This confirmation was actually quite heady stuff, although it had the disadvantage of fixing me still further in the role of little orphan Abey: every light casts a shadow.

I pulled myself together. As a grown man in his late thirties, I wasn't up for playing a poverty stricken orphan for long.

"It's okay. It's just one of those things. You do have to remember that I'm likely to be oversensitive about secrets. My family has always been one huge secret and growing up without knowing who you are isn't all sweetness and light."

"Yes, I forget that," she said thoughtfully. "I take for granted my knowledge and my memories. I carry my story with me at all times. You have to write yours as you go along." That was an interesting way to phrase things, but this was no time to quibble with her choice of words and, anyway, it also rang true with me somehow. It certainly served to smooth down any remaining ruffled feathers I might have had, and dinner came and went without any further tensions. The wine was extremely good, the food was at least as good as the wine, and the company was excellent. The more time I spent with Eve, the more it felt as if I had always known her, which I recognise is something of a cliché, but maybe the foolishness of falling in love makes you think and talk like that. Borders and boundaries start to crumble, words flow away, and you are left scrabbling for concepts you would have been ashamed to admit to only a few hours before.

* * *

By the time we had finished our meal, several bottles of wine had been emptied, and it was very late. Eve spoke to the waiter and then turned to me.

"Okay, Abraham, are you going to escort me home safely?"

I was surprised by this for two reasons: one, because she had called me Abraham and two, because she didn't seem like the sort of woman to need a man to escort her home. This, therefore, seemed like a no frills request to go home with her, which was a surprise, albeit a very welcome one. I hadn't realised that the evening had gone so well. First things first, though.

"Err, why have you just called me Abraham?" I asked.

"Isn't it your full name?" She now seemed as surprised as me. "I mean, everyone calls you Abe. You've repeatedly said your name is Old Testament, and you've wondered if you are Jewish. I just assumed it was Abraham. I didn't mean to offend. I just wanted to try it out in full; there isn't much scope for shortening Abe any further, so lengthening it seemed like the next best thing. Your full name is Abraham, right?"

"Um, wrong, actually."

"So what is it, actually?"

"Best carry on calling me Abe. Everyone does."

"I know. I've been calling you Abe, but I wanted to customise it somehow and not just do as everyone else does. This evening seemed the right time to make things more personal. Anyway, now you are the one keeping a secret. What is your full name?"

I paused. It wasn't a secret. I was just embarrassed by it: a leftover from childhood. I hesitated, but there was no point in keeping it from her.

"Abel. My name is Abel, as in Cain and Abel."

She seemed somehow pleased. Or was it just amused? "So what's wrong with Abel? It's a good name."

"Nothing. I took a lot of ribbing about it when I was a kid. The biblical connotations seemed to be an endless source of amusement for some of my peers, especially as Abel was famous for having a brother, and I managed to have no family whatsoever. It became a bit of a raw nerve, I guess."

"Well, I am truly sorry for hitting that nerve, however unintentionally. But, Abel, I would still very much appreciate a safe escort home. It's late, I have drunk rather a lot of good wine, and your company on the tube and after would be good. Do you mind?" She leant on the words *and after.* "What could I say?

"I should be delighted to escort you home, m'lady," I said, offering my arm in what I hoped was a chivalrous gesture, as well as a clear indication that any embarrassment was now over. It also meant that we walked to the tube station arm in arm, remained linked together on the train, and arrived at an imposing white-fronted house near Regents Park even more closely entwined.

Given the family connection with the property, you might have thought I would take some interest in the building, that I would be looking for further clues as to the family legacy, or even that I would be anticipating a sense of recognition, of coming home. But no, my thoughts, such as they were, were very much elsewhere.

"Night cap?" she asked, and I couldn't refuse.

I did notice that the house was grand, as evidenced by the entrance hall, which was very understatedly luxurious in a dark wood, antique sort of way. But just at this moment, I was not really interested in undertaking a review of its interior design. We bypassed the pseudo-baroque delights of the drawing room and the possibility of night caps all together and went straight up the staircase and into Eve's bedroom, where I spent the night in crisp luxury linen sheets and luxuriously soft, long dark hair.

XI

How do I describe the next morning and the day that followed other than as a glorious physical blur? Actually, I am not sure I want to try. It was perfect. It was private. We made love, we had sex, we fucked, we made love again, and then more agains. Eve was all sorts of wonderful; she was imaginative, demanding, rewardingly supple. Eve was outstanding. She was my most extreme exotic sexual fantasy and then some. Those dreams that had been draining me dry not so long before were pallid precursors to her full Technicolor majesty. You get the picture. Or, rather, you don't, because the images and memories are staying firmly within my head: mine, all mine alone.

I left the Regents Park house late on Sunday morning, as Eve had an appointment for Sunday lunch that she couldn't break. I felt light-headed. I felt exhausted. I felt like I was King of the World.

Thoughts of family, thoughts of possible wealth, had gone out the window. The only thing that mattered now was Eve. In just under a week, she had become central to my existence, yet I had passed the whole of my life up to now without ever feeling that way about anybody. If miracles were not, inevitably, namby-pamby, holier-than-thou events necessarily involving some kind of God, or at least an emissary of one, I would have said it was a miracle.

I survived the rest of Sunday without her and managed to spend the next day at work, as in I was physically located at my place of work, but my heart, head, spirit, and libido were all most definitely elsewhere. I only got through the day because I knew we were going to meet up again that night. Once more, the evening was to begin with dinner at the candle-lit La Luna; she didn't seem interested in going anywhere else, but as I was only interested in her, I didn't mind where we met. Menu diversity was not important to me.

After dinner that night, we ended up at my flat. Despite Eve's grand Central London address, she had no objections to slumming it when it came to sleeping arrangements, not that sleeping, as such, took up much of our time. At that stage in the evening, we were so totally wrapped up, in, around and inside one another, that venue was not an issue. I can see her now, naked, spread-eagled unselfconsciously across my bed, her face and arms covered by the sheet, her breasts just peeking from underneath it, and her belly and genitals displayed for me, her slit dark and inflamed: the secret origin of my new-found world.

She had to leave early the next morning because of business commitments, but left behind her a promise to meet up again on Thursday night and then spend the whole of Friday with me. I booked my leave from the paper in sweating anticipation.

The week crawled sluggishly towards Thursday evening. The intervening days were flat and uneventful. I worked, I slept, and comfortingly, I dreamed. Not the hallucinatory porno-fantasies of before, with the physical manifestations that had so revolted Jenny; these dreams were also vivid and graphic, but wove themselves around Eve in glorious, intimate, and realistic detail. They kept me company until Thursday night.

We had already established our own routine: dinner at La Luna with a bottle of the house special and then bed. I enjoyed just being with Eve, but after the dreams of the previous two nights I was impatient to get to the bed stage of the evening. Thursday night's dinner, as good as it undoubtedly was, seemed to take an age, and the four stops on the way back to Regents Park station felt like the ultimate London Underground go slow. Eventually, we got back to her house and bedroom, and for me, the night then began in earnest. Her body flowed like a river: streaming long black hair, softly undulating curves of flesh and the shadowy pool of thick primal curls at the confluence of her legs with its promise of moist, waiting depths. I dived deep and lost myself within her.

* * *

I woke up the next morning in eager anticipation of the day to come. I had a strange sense of urgency and the need to cram as much as possible in to our day together. I was, therefore, taken aback to find Eve already up and dressed.

"I'm sorry, Abel, it's very annoying, but I have to go out for a bit."

I was even more taken aback. "Why? I thought we had agreed we were going to spend the whole day together." I could hear the petulance in my voice. I was the five-year-old who has just been told that the promised trip to the park this morning has been cancelled.

"We can still have most of today together. It's just that I have to pop out for a couple of hours this morning on business. I'll be as quick as I can, and I'll come straight back."

My inner five-year-old still wanted to go to the park this morning. "But why do you have to go now? Why can't it wait? This was supposed to be our day. If it's that important, why are you only telling me now?"

Eve was very reasonable. "I have only just found out now."

I raised my eyebrows at this. I hadn't heard any phones ring, and although I had slept through her getting up, I felt irrationally sure she hadn't gone anywhere beyond the bedroom and its adjoining bathroom.

"Oh Abel, sweetie, don't get stroppy. There was a text on my Blackberry. I had it on silent, so we didn't hear it come through, but I saw the text once I woke up."

"But why now? Why can't it wait?" My inner child was determined not to be placated.

"It's important. Someone I've been waiting to make contact with has just turned up, and I need to meet with them as soon as possible. It really should only take a couple of hours. Then we'll have the rest of the day together, and you could stay over tonight. We could have tomorrow together as well. What do you think?"

The standard ploy with young children; if they won't accept that they can't have what they want, bribe them with something bigger and better. The trouble was, my rediscovered child was set on going to the park now, this instant, and no promises of a longer trip in the future, even with added ice cream, were going to placate him.

"Fine. So, what do you expect me to do whilst you are out?"

Eve smiled. "Well, you could just rest up and recharge your batteries, lover. That could pay huge dividends when I come back." I didn't return her smile. "Or you could linger over a nice breakfast downstairs and then explore the books in the library. There is quite a reasonable collection, you know. Quite unusual too. You'd enjoy it." With that she picked up her bag, kissed me firmly and decisively on the mouth and walked out of the room.

I sat there in silence and listened to Eve walk down the stairs. I was still sitting there when I heard the front door shut. My inner spoilt brat was, by now, quite upset. She had chosen to go; she hadn't chosen to stay with me. How could she just walk out like that when she knew I wanted her to stay? Things between us had been going so well, were so new and addictive that I simply couldn't understand how she could leave so calmly, walking away from us and the plans we had made without a trace of reluctance. I am not too proud to admit that I sat there and sulked for some time, but eventually the adult in me took at least partial control, and I decided to go downstairs to find breakfast.

The organisation of the house was actually quite impressive. I had never seen any servants or staff around the property, possibly because most of my time had been spent in Eve's bed, but the house ran discreetly like a handmade Swiss clock. Everything was always where it needed to be, when it needed to be there. When I went downstairs that morning, the breakfast table looked freshly laid with hot steaming coffee, scrambled eggs, and warm toast. It can only have been recently prepared, but I had neither heard nor seen its preparation. The smell of coffee was enticing, and for once, the taste was almost as good as the aroma. I ate a good breakfast, determined to enjoy myself in spite of Eve's untimely and thoughtless absence.

With breakfast out of the way, I decided to have a good look, not just at the library, but at the whole property. In my several trips to the house, I had really only seen the hall, the staircase, and Eve's bedroom with its adjoining bathroom. I was curious to see the rest of Eve's home and what it told me about her. Then, there was the issue of family. Would there be any trace of a heritage that I could possibly call mine, that might hint at who I was? I was also pettily intrigued to find out how many servants there actually were and where they managed to secrete themselves so successfully whilst keeping the house running to order.

Breakfast had been served in what I assumed was the dining room. I went from there out into the hallway and decided to begin my explorations with the downstairs rooms, working through them all in an anti-clockwise fashion, and then moving onto the first and second floors in due course.

The house was surprisingly large, or at least larger than I had assumed based on the street frontage. The rooms were all classily furnished: discreet luxury in a classic style, and with a number of very choice antiques. The overall effect was tasteful Victorian opulence, if such a thing is possible, and unostentatiously displayed wealth. Despite the primarily nineteenth century feel, many of the best pieces in the house were actually much older. Needless to say, they must have been worth a few bob.

On the ground floor of the building, in addition to the dining room, there was the lounge, the drawing room (basically, a second lounge for posh people), the spacious hall, a domestic back area, which looked sizeable in its own right, and a library.

The library was large and very Victorian in style: all dark wood panelling and well-polished brass work with deep red, expensively thick, sound-swallowing, wool carpet. Eve was right, there was a good collection of books, eclectic and wide ranging in choice, including a sizeable collection of expensively bound antiquarian books and manuscripts in a thick glass-fronted case. Everything in the library was spotlessly clean and lovingly polished, but I still hadn't seen or heard anyone else in the house since Eve left. Out of growing curiosity, I therefore decided to head to the back of the house, where I assumed I would find the kitchen and utility areas and the individual, or individuals, who must spend their time keeping everything just so.

The kitchen was large, well equipped and modern; so far the only exception to the antique styling in the rest of the house. It gleamed with a lot of stainless steel and spotless glass. Despite the relatively recent preparation of my breakfast, it looked as if it had never actually been used, and there was no sign of anyone's presence other than mine. Whoever the hired help were, they were extremely efficient and extraordinarily discreet.

I completed my tour of the other ground floor rooms and returned to the dining room where I had earlier had my breakfast, only to find that during my walkabout, the breakfast things had been spirited away. This was silly. There had to be at least one other person in the house apart from me, but we hadn't met up once. I went back to the kitchen area yelling "hello" very loudly, but there was no reply and no sound of movement other than my own. I called out again asking for another cup of coffee that I knew I didn't really want, but there was still no response.

I decided to undertake a quick tour of the upstairs rooms in case whoever else was in the house had gone up there and therefore couldn't hear me, although this did seem rather unlikely. Each room was as tastefully furnished as the last, and every surface was spotless and well polished, but the phantom polisher was nowhere to be found. I ended up jogging through the rooms in case the apparent cleaning obsessive was also moving through the rooms in parallel with me as they hunted down every last speck of dust in the house. I found no one, although when I came to Eve's bedroom, I wasn't surprised to find that the signs of our night-time passion had been discreetly tidied up with fresh sheets placed on the now precisely made bed.

I went back downstairs and repeated my jogging approach through the downstairs rooms I had only recently visited, but I failed to find any signs of life. This was perplexing. The house seemed deserted, apart from me, and yet there was obviously at least one other person moving around the property, so why couldn't I find them? Then it occurred to me that a house of this size and age was bound to have a cellar, and it was likely that once down there they would not be able to hear me, and I wouldn't hear them. I hadn't previously seen an obvious cellar entrance, but then I hadn't been specifically looking for one. I wasn't sure I was intentionally being avoided, but it was almost becoming a matter of pride for me that I should track down this fellow individual to say hello. I resumed my circuit of the ground floor, this time looking for a cellar entrance and therefore opening every door I could find, including those I had previously dismissed as cupboard doors.

In the drawing room, I found a small door that had obviously been artfully designed to blend in with the wall décor. I wouldn't claim that it was a secret door, but it was an intentionally unobtrusive one. I opened it gently to find myself staring into a gloomy narrow cupboard, which in itself was hardly surprising. The cupboard's contents were, however, another matter altogether. As I opened the door fully, a picture light at the back of the cupboard came on to illuminate the almost life-size eighteenth century portrait that hung there: a portrait of a youngish woman with dark hair and eyes wearing a midnight blue velvet empire-line dress. It was Lily.

I stood there, just staring. Then I stared some more. What was the painting doing in a cupboard and, more confusingly, what was it doing in a cupboard in Eve's house when, on several occasions that I could remember, she had denied all knowledge of this very picture? How could she not know about it when she appeared to actually own it?

Once I had got over the initial shock, I checked the painting over thoroughly. As far as I could tell from a layman's point of view, it was the original that I had seen in a London gallery all those years ago. Like the rest of the house, it had been extremely well maintained and scrupulously cleaned. This wasn't going to turn out to be a long lost family heirloom that everyone had forgotten. So I returned, reluctantly in many ways, to my original question: what was it doing here and why had Eve denied all knowledge of it?

The surprise of suddenly coming across Lily in a cupboard distracted me from my previous obsession of trying to meet up with the household staff. Instead, I just sat in stupefied amazement in front of the open cupboard door and directly opposite the illuminated Lily, drinking in every detail of her. It was, I assume, like coming across a long-lost love or, more appropriately in my case, a long-lost relative. It was my Lily. I hadn't imagined her or remembered her wrongly. She really did exist. It was just that I had never in a month of Sundays expected to find her here and like this.

Through the fog of shock, it slowly started to dawn on me that I was going to have to confront Eve over this. She had twice denied all knowledge of Lily, and yet here Lily was, safe and illuminated within her own personal closet. At best, Eve had a lot of explaining to do, although I was buggered if I could come up with a plausible reason for her denial of Lily or the painting's presence here; at worst she had lied to me. That hardly boded well for our nascent relationship, however passionate.

The more I gnawed this over, the more I knew in my heart of hearts that this was not a positive thing, but I also knew equally strongly that I didn't want anything to get in the way of my relationship with Eve. What we had, the bond we had already forged, was so primal that I could not imagine being without it. Nothing could be allowed to weaken it, absolutely nothing, and with that thought uppermost in my head, I quietly shut the cupboard door and waited for Eve to return home.

As I waited, the shock of finding Lily abated slightly and the need to challenge Eve about it became less pressing. I didn't forget about it. It just seemed to slide away from the forefront of my mind, allowing other thoughts to take centre stage. In particular, my need for Eve seemed to grow, along with a barely conscious imperative to look after her and safeguard our relationship at all costs. I found myself thinking how much I missed her. I became anxious once more over her sudden departure and kept wondering how long it would be before she came back. Her absence became more and more uncomfortable as the minutes ticked away. It was like a constant itch in my head and an ache in other more demanding parts of my body, so that when, not that much later, she walked back in through the front door, my only conscious thought was to grab hold of her firmly, sweep her up into my arms, and carry her back upstairs to bed. I hadn't totally forgotten about Lily, but the physical urge to be part of Eve had become so much more important than anything else that she would just have to wait.

* * *

When I finally surfaced from a deep avalanche of snow white sheets and erotically stifling night-black hair, I knew there was something I needed to ask Eve, but I couldn't for the life of me remember what it was. Just as I started, ever so slightly, to struggle with this, Eve dropped a bombshell which deafened every other thought in my mind.

"Abel, I have to tell you this. I don't want to, but I have to go away for a while. I mean really away. Abroad. For a bit. Well, for more than a bit. For a few weeks actually. I'm so sorry, but I do have to go".

For the second time that day, although I no longer realised it at the time, I sat stupefied. Eve was always saying sorry, but it didn't stop her from hurting me. This time she was leaving me, going away, not choosing to be with me, but choosing to be somewhere else. The where didn't matter; it was the not here, the not with me, that did. The air had been sucked out of my lungs. I was more than inconsolable. Life suddenly seemed impossible. I struggled to say something, to not cry. It was only for a fortnight or so. This was stupid. I was a grown man, for goodness sake. I should be in control of my emotions, but I no longer knew how to be.

Eve, as ever, seemed to have been reading my mind. Very slowly and clearly, as if to a small child, she said,

"I am not leaving you, Abel. That is not the reason for my going. I don't want to go, and I will come back. For you. But first, I have to go. You will forgive me, won't you? Forgive me and wait for me. Please." She came over to me and held me in her arms, cupping my head to her soft, warm breasts. "It is only for two or so weeks, and then I will be back. It can be as if I had never been away." She was crying now, and so was I. I tried to kiss her tears away, despite my own, and we sank back down into the avalanche and became lost in it, imminent separation adding to the urgency of our need for one another.

I was inhaling her. Her skin smelled of warm earth, jasmine and long, dark nights after the heat of a sun-bathed day. Consuming her. Her skin tasting of both honey and salt, making me remember a cocktail I'd once had, sometime back, beyond the importance of now. It didn't matter when, but the cocktail had been perfect. Perfect like

Eve's sculpted body, as I ran my hands over her curves, feeling all of her, every smooth and flawless inch. Then, exploring more intimately in increasingly focussed motions. Repeating. Rediscovering. Delving. So perfect a body, it could have belonged to the craft of Rodin. But it didn't, it belonged to me. I parted her warm flesh with my own, immersing myself in her heat. She arched her back to receive me, and I pushed down deeper and deeper, taking her with me until I broke through into oblivion.

Eventually, we had to come back up for air, and I knew that if I wanted to preserve what little was left of my dignity, I just had to pull on my clothes and go before we started talking again. Eve seemed to understand this and silently watched me get dressed. I kept telling myself that I was over-reacting, that this wasn't the end of the world. It was just for a short while, and so strong a primal bond as Eve and I had would easily survive that. None of this really helped though. Somehow, I got myself out of the house by concentrating on our recent passion and the memory of its heat in an attempt to convince myself that all would be okay. But by the time I arrived back at my empty flat, it felt as if the whole of my world had caved in, and I was alone in its rubble, suffocating in the dark.

It was over forty-eight hours later and some time after Eve's flight had left Heathrow that the memory of Lily came back into my head, and I simultaneously realised that I had not confronted Eve over the matter of the painting, that I could not actually recall where Eve was going, nor precisely why, and that I did not have any way of contacting her other than her mobile phone.

XII

The first week of Eve's absence passed me by in a grey smog of depression and flu-like complaints. When not at home feeling really ill, I kept myself busy. I made myself go into work regardless of symptoms. Work expanded to fill the void left by Eve, and when not tied down by the demands of paid work, I continued to write, which, for me, is always a good way to make sense of things. Writing started off as a useful activity to keep me occupied and take my mind off the aches, pains, and night sweats that I was going through, but the process enabled me to lose myself amongst the words and helped to clear my mind, making space for my thoughts to stretch out. As my head returned to normal, it surprised me just how cluttered my thinking had become. Often, it is only when things begin to get better that you can really estimate just how bad they've been. As for why I was like this, I didn't know. Feeling down after Eve's sudden departure was natural. I had no grounds for going cold-turkey, so the sweats were probably some kind of virus. Put the two together, and maybe that was why my thought processes had more holes than a lump of Swiss cheese in a busy rat run.

Not resting didn't help much to improve my physical or mental state, either. When I fell asleep, the nightmares of my childhood crept back home, together with the lurid hallucinations of the Jenny period. If I managed to sleep, I was either falling for all eternity into the eyes of an owl-like moon or my dreams were triple x-rated, and this time round there was very little pleasure to be had from them. I am sure that most men (and presumably a number of women) will find that hard to believe. Once upon a time, I would have felt the same way, but if you have seen Kubrick's *A Clockwork Orange*, just contemplate for a nightmare of moments Little Alex's fix, and then you may have some idea of how I felt. Once inside my dreams, there was no let up and no escape. To make matters even more uncomfortable, Eve was now a regular actress within these lurid extravaganzas. Yet, rather than recreate the sensual exoticism of my earlier fantasies, these grubby manifestations managed to cheapen and debase the actual pleasure they fed from. Difficult to appreciate, I know, but nevertheless true. This was way beyond normal top-shelf porn and darker than any heavy duty pornography I had ever come across. Each time I woke up feeling somehow sordid and unclean. Sleep, therefore, was hardly resting or restorative, and it was not at all surprising that my subconscious resisted falling into the arms of Morpheus in the first place, sensing, as it did, what waited within them. What was surprising was that, as the week progressed, I started to feel increasingly clear-headed in spite of minimal sleep and apparent ill health.

Contact with Eve at such distance had been limited: a few brief text messages, the odd snatched conversation, and increasingly terse voice messages. She never seemed to answer her phone when it rang, or the signal, wherever she was, was poor, so I texted or left brief messages for her. She, in turn, called me rarely, and then in the dead of night when my phone was off in a vain attempt to get some sort of sleep, so she was obliged to leave voice messages for me. There was no proper communication and no opportunity to raise difficult questions.

With the increasing clarity of life seen through the rear-view mirror, I realised that what I didn't know about Eve and her family (or should that be our family, I wasn't even really sure of that) was far greater than what I did know. The headlong fall into passion and distraction seemed to have taken precedence over the search for my roots and the many questions I wanted, or perhaps should have expected, to have answered. Now, that Eve was not around to tangle up my thoughts in her long black hair, I found that I knew very little of substance. It came back to me, however, that she had lied to me about the painting of Lily, but I still didn't know why.

* * *

In Eve's second week away, my aches and sweats began to improve, and I spent a few days attempting to research the story of Eve Striga in more detail, but I found myself paddling in the shallows rather than bathing in deeper waters as expected. As ever, what I didn't know exceeded what I did.

L. Striga was recorded as the sole resident and owner of the house near Regents Park. L. Eve Striga of the same address was shown as the sole proprietor of La Luna Restaurant, which, it turns out, is at the same address once less reputably occupied by the Black Moon Club, and subsequently a Chinese takeaway and restaurant. Surprising, therefore, that Eve was unaware of this. Knowing Eve's attention to detail, I found it hard to credit that she didn't know what had been occupying the site before she set up La Luna on it. In addition to this, Eve Striga had been, for the last eighteen months, a patron of the art gallery where we first met. And that, basically, was that. If she had any other business interests, I couldn't find them. If she carried out any other public or charitable works, she was exceedingly low-key about them. Search for "Striga" on the Internet and you will find screens of agricultural and botanical sites on the subject of Witchweed (botanical name: *Striga*) which, with its pretty pink flowers, is slowly stifling and squeezing the life out of essential African crops. Search further and, apart from a solicitor in Athens, you may find a few references to east European witchcraft or barn owls, but there is no trace of Eve. For a lady with apparently a good deal of money, she was very, very low profile. So, too, were the rest of the family, whoever they might be. This didn't feel entirely natural. I confess, I was starting to have some doubts about my new-found lady friend and even beginning to query some of the things she had told me.

Don't get me wrong. I hadn't fallen out of love with Eve, but I had started to float back into the clearer waters of reality from the bottomless depths of initial infatuation. When Eve returned, there were questions that needed to be answered, but first, and before she arrived back at the house, I intended to attempt some further practical research of my own.

XIII

The night before Eve returned, I slept like a baby and, for once, a baby that wasn't in fear of drowning in the eternal gaze of a small, brown owl. For the first time in a month, I awoke feeling truly refreshed. Ironically, therefore, I phoned in sick and absented myself from the paper for the day. Fortunately, they had grown used to it.

I had things to do. Eve had texted me briefly with her plans, saying she would be back that afternoon and had later phoned me for a few stilted moments to suggest that I come round to her house at three o'clock. I, however, intended to arrive somewhat earlier than that.

I was outside the house just after midday. If Eve was hoping to see me just as soon as she got back home, which she had assured me she was, and based on the rest of our most recent conversation, which, despite being brief, was the longest we had had in over two weeks, I estimated her actual arrival time back at the house at just gone two at the absolute earliest. That gave me well over an hour to look around, assuming there was someone in the house to let me in early and willing to do so. I had come up with a variety of reasons to explain to the member of Eve's staff who answered the door why I had arrived so early and why I needed to wait for Eve inside, rather than go away and come back again. As it was, I needn't have bothered.

When I got to the house, with its perfect and imposing Portland Stone façade, the front door appeared shut, so I rang the bell and waited. I rang the bell again. No answer. It looked as if I wasn't going to see the elusive member of staff after all. I rang a third time, and when there was still no response, I applied a skill I had acquired at the children's home all those years back and picked the lock. Some things you just don't forget. I had originally been worried that breaking in via the front door in full daylight would leave me rather exposed, but the lock gave way easily. Eve's locksmith was clearly not up to scratch. It was amazing that she hadn't been burgled before this. This was London. I hoped her insurance was good. Anyway, you take the chances you are given in life, so I walked straight in.

Once inside, I checked the back of the house, including the kitchen, followed by Eve's bedroom area. All seemed well. It did not seem as if Eve had returned unexpectedly early and, as ever, there was no sign of anyone else. This still gave me an hour or so, as I reckoned, to carry out a bit of research, starting with the cupboards and drawers in Eve's room and then, if nothing was helpful there, working outwards and down through the main areas of the house. If challenged, I was looking for something I had left behind when I was last here, but deep down, I really wasn't expecting to come across anyone.

The bedroom produced nothing much of interest. A few of Eve's clothes were hanging in the wardrobe: all expensive designer labels, no Marks & Spencers. The same went for what clothing was left in the drawers. Her toiletries were still in the bathroom, along with the usual paraphernalia of hairbrushes, hairdryer and the like. There were no documents or photographs or uniquely personal affects that I could find — lots of intimate stuff that you would expect to find in someone's room, but all somehow impersonal. It could have belonged to any woman, or at least any woman with money.

The other rooms on the first floor were either bedrooms or bathrooms. I couldn't recall seeing a study or similar space on the second floor during my jog around on my last day here, so I decided that downstairs was the best place to look for something that might give me some more background on Eve or her family. I also wanted some time with Lily before Eve came back.

The drawing room was, as ever, spotless and looked unlived in, like a show home. Any ornaments in the room were most definitely antique. The paintings on the wall looked expensive. They were all landscapes or still life — not a portrait amongst them. The books on the coffee table were all of a type produced to lie on the coffee tables of the wealthy and chic, and they did what they were designed to do very well, but they told me little about Eve, personally. The room contained no photographs, no obviously personal books or objects, and no papers of any sort. A thorough check revealed only the one partially concealed cupboard and that was the one with Lily in it.

I opened the door and Lily was flooded by light. The sight of her still made me take a sharp intake of breath. I didn't know how I had managed to stay away from her for so long. She was so very beautiful, and so was my mother, and so, of course, was Eve. My response to the painting served to emphasise the fact that meeting up with Eve again was not going to be that easy, not if I intended to be purely logical and focused. I side stepped the thought as I had side stepped so many others in the last month. There are none so blind as those that choose to wear exceedingly dark glasses. One thing at a time, though. I still had things to do before my reunion with Eve. I basked in Lily's beauty for a few minutes more and then slowly and reluctantly consigned her once more to the dark, as I shut the door before heading across the hall to the dining room and the library.

The dining room boasted yet more landscape painting, non-concealed cupboards of glassware, cutlery and crockery, some more tasteful antiques, and a very large vase of fresh lilies. Their scent was filling the room and was stealthily beginning to make its way out into the hall, but it hadn't quite got there yet. Someone had been in the house recently, but there was still no sign of them, which was fine as far as I was concerned.

Although the dining room had yielded nothing of real use to me, I had higher hopes of the library which, apart from shelves and shelves of books and papers, contained a large desk and had the potential to double as Eve's study. I had therefore earmarked the library for the most painstaking search of my ongoing investigations.

The desk did seem to be Eve's personal one, but the only papers it contained were a few household bills for food and flowers, some of her business cards, and plain, unused stationery. There was no computer and no obviously personal documents. To make sure I didn't miss anything, I emptied all the desk drawers, checked shelves, even looked in books for scribbled comments or dates, but there was nothing personal, nothing which gave me a real clue as to who Eve was.

* * *

By now, I had spent over an hour in the house, and I was nervously conscious of Eve's imminent return, as well as the fact that someone other than me had been in the house relatively recently to do the flowers in the dining room and might therefore still be around or about to come back. I was wondering whether to leave the house, take a turn 'round the park for a bit and then come back, all above board, at the agreed time, when it occurred to me that, despite my intensive rummaging through almost all of the library, I hadn't thought to look in the glass fronted cabinet that contained the library's antiquarian volumes. I had assumed it would be locked, but I hadn't actually tried it, and this struck me as rather a serious oversight on my part, given that a locked cabinet would be an ideal place to store important personal documents, which so far had been conspicuous by their absence from the house.

I walked over to the cabinet and gently pulled on one of the glass-fronted doors, expecting it to remain firmly shut. To my surprise, it opened. Eve's security arrangements were really appallingly lax. I pulled on its partner door and, with due respect to the apparent age of some of the manuscripts, started to go through the contents. A quick perusal of the titles that were legible seemed to indicate that the works were primarily religious. The title that immediately caught my eye was *The Book of Abel*; your own name always manages to shriek louder than any surrounding text. It was clearly part of a larger collection. There were a good many other editions of the same book and what also appeared to be a number of foreign language versions of it. Some manuscripts were untitled and some were in languages and alphabets I couldn't read, but the more I looked, the more it seemed as if every book whose title I could at least partially make out dealt with my namesake. How odd was that? With such a striking mono-themed collection in her library, one might have thought that Eve would have made some mention of it once she had learned my name. The fact that she hadn't was added to the ever-growing list of queries to be addressed.

I took down the first book that had grabbed my attention, *The Book of Abel*, and was just about to open it when I thought I heard something. I froze and waited. There was no repeat of the sound, but it made me less than comfortable. If I was caught in the house by someone, I had my story lined up about looking for something I had lost on my last visit, but it wouldn't really explain away my rummaging in the oldest and presumably most expensive part of Eve's book collection. There had already been more than enough veiled comments about family wealth and my motivations in relation to it, as far as I was concerned. The books weren't what I had come for, anyway. I had wanted to discover the real Eve, but had failed. There was nothing of her I could grasp. Her presence was like smoke, and in her absence, it had dissipated.

As per the rest of the house, there appeared to be no personal papers or indications as to Eve's past in the bookcase, either. I gently put the book back in its place and slowly and quietly began to shut the cabinet doors. There was that noise again — muffled but seemingly closer. I was starting to feel edgily uncomfortable now; that feeling you get when someone is staring at you without you consciously knowing it. I finished closing the glass doors and began to turn. I almost made a noise myself when I caught sight of a face reflected in the glass of the door panel. For a moment, I thought there was someone standing behind me. Then I recognised my own face staring back at me. The glass in the cabinet was old and obviously distorted. It gave my look of surprise an air of wildness and had the distracting effect of giving me a blemish on my forehead, right between my eyes. The mark was probably an overlaid reflection of something else, but as I moved my head to change the angle of distortion and clarify what I was actually seeing, the whole image jumped away. When I repositioned myself to catch sight of my reflection once more, the mark was no longer visible.

Then I heard a noise again, and it dawned on me that playing catch-as-catch-can with my own reflection was hardly adult and far from sensible if I was about to be caught in the act. I made an effort to remember myself, but there appeared to be no one actually present to notice my return to rational behaviour.

I checked my watch. It was almost two; how time flies when you are snooping illicitly around someone else's house. I had real justification for my jumpiness. Given my guesstimate that Eve could be arriving back anytime from two onwards, I had already outstayed my lack of welcome and was cutting it extremely fine if I was going to opt for plan B (improvised on the spot when I realised that there was no one in the house but me) and go back out of the front door, take a walk in the park and return at three, as arranged. I was risking bumping into Eve on her way in and that would take some very creative story-telling on my part.

I decided to adopt a new, equally spontaneous plan C, which involved the manufacture of another excuse for my being in the house before she was. Specifically, I was going to say that I was so eager to see her after a fortnight's absence, I had got to the house early, which was true, had found the door on the latch, which wasn't, and had decided to wait inside for her, which was almost, with a little bit of a side-step, close to the truth. I was obviously going to omit the bit about investigating every interesting nook and cranny of her house whilst I was waiting, but that was an omission rather than an outright lie. I always find that stories work best when what you say contains at least some recognisable truths; it makes for less work and creates an easier aura of credibility. Moreover, part of the art of story telling, as I see it, is as much about what you leave out as what you actually tell. I just hoped the latch part of my story wouldn't get the flower arranger into too much trouble, but with such weak security to begin with, it seemed unlikely and might at least cause Eve to review her security arrangements, which had to be a good thing.

I decided to wait for Eve in the drawing room. To be seen to be whiling away the time in an appropriate manner, I settled myself on a well-upholstered settee and started to browse through the upmarket coffee table books. Despite my jitteriness, it was a pleasant enough way of passing the time: sitting in a comfortable and well-appointed room, looking at beautiful images whilst surrounded by the almost overpowering smell of fresh lilies. I was surprised I hadn't noticed the lilies before, as they were in a vase at least as grand as that in the dining room, but I did not have much time to ponder this oversight, as I heard the front door open and the sound of Eve's heels on the hallway floor.

I could feel the adrenaline starting to surge, and despite myself, I stood up and walked over to the drawing room door to welcome her home.

She was standing just inside the front door, a dark grey silk dress clinging to her skin and accentuating every curve of her outline. Seeing her again was like coming across the painting of Lily. Eve's beauty hit me like a blow to the solar plexus, and it was all I could do to turn the resultant gasp into a more discrete, if still sharp, intake of breath and lily fumes. I wanted to grab hold of her, kiss her fully on the mouth, carry her upstairs and lose myself so deep within her that it hurt. All my thoughts were rushing so single-mindedly towards this possibility and the pleasure coming after, that it took the little self control I had remaining to remind my consciousness that, as much as I loved her and wanted her, I didn't actually trust her, and there were now rather a lot of unanswered questions between us.

Whilst I had paused in an attempt to regain at least some command of self and thoughts, Eve caught sight of me and after an initial look of surprise, dropped her bags, ran over to me, and threw her arms around my neck. I inhaled her along with the lilies.

"Abel! You're here early. How lovely!" She kissed me thoroughly, very thoroughly, and it was as if she was sucking all rational thought out of my head. I was now only conscious of her, her mouth, her breasts with their hard little nipples, her whole supple body pressed into mine, and the intoxicating, musky smell of her blending with the aroma of lilies. I was drowning, and when I finally came up for air, I was not surprised to find we were already in her bedroom and pulling off one another's clothes.

XIV

I surfaced slowly from the deep, deep pool of slaked desire that I had been floating in, deep down where there is no time and no now, no conscious thought and therefore no reality. It is both a physical state and an absence of one, all sensation and none, a case of simultaneously being and not being. I was gradually returning to an elemental level of existence. First, I became aware of my own extremities and then Eve's limbs wrapped around them. I was either deliriously happy or happily delirious, and yet, as conscious thought slowly reasserted its right to at least part of my brain, I was becoming aware of an uncertain sense of disquiet, a vague feeling that there was something I should have done, or maybe said, that I hadn't. I didn't know what it was and whatever it was, if it meant a drastic change from my current state, I didn't want to know. Nevertheless, I couldn't shift my growing sense of semiconscious discomfort.

Eve stirred next to me and stretched. I could feel her skin and its warm underlying flesh rubbing and pressing against mine. It was smooth and soft and wonderfully arousing, and I rolled over to take hold of Eve all over again, but she gently, yet decisively, rolled away from me and got out of bed.

"Now, now, be a good boy," she said. "They'll be plenty of time for more later. Right now, though, I need to tell you what I've found out while I have been away."

Away. Yes, she had been away, and that had been bad, but now she was back. That was impossibly good, and therefore, away no longer mattered. It was as if it had never happened, and all those stupid negative doubts and suspicions that I had during that awful period could simply now evaporate with the sweat of our love making. I wouldn't have to worry about them ever again.

"Come on sweetie. Pay attention. I need to tell you what I've been up to." She was persistent in wanting to talk, but if that was what she wanted to do, then that was okay by me. I just wanted to be with her and to make her happy. That was the only thing that had ever mattered.

Eve sat on the edge of the bed and took hold of my hand. Her hair was cascading across her shoulders like the waves of a midnight sea.

"At least I put our regrettable time apart to good use," she was saying. "It gave me the opportunity to do some family research. I've dug up some useful information, but I'm afraid it's rather worrying, too." Her dark hair was running over her white skin like rivulets of black coffee spreading through fresh cream. "Abel, listen to me. This is important."

Abel. I knew that word. Why was Abel important? Then it clicked. Abel was my name, was who I was. I had found some books. Shelves and shelves of them. They had been trying to tell me my name too.

Eve was still talking. Her voice wafted around my ears without actually resonating within them. What had books got to do with me? Books in a cupboard. I'd seen something else in a cupboard recently. As I struggled to work out what, Lily came back to me out of the dark. Beautiful Lily, as beautiful as Eve, but Eve had denied knowing about her sublime beauty, despite evidence to the contrary. Then, there were those books — a collection of Abels all screaming my name at me at once. Concern started to creep into my head like cold water trickling through slowly widening cracks. A large collection of books on Abel in her library, and Eve, whose lover is called Abel, doesn't think to mention it at all, not even in passing? This from the same woman who had a concealed painting in a cupboard that she had denied all knowledge of and whose own personal footprint in the world had to-date proved unusually slight. If I was still largely oblivious to external sounds, the warning bells within my head were starting to tinkle a little, just a little, maybe, but I finally had to admit that something wasn't right.

"You aren't listening to me, are you?" Eve was still trying to tell me what she had been doing, but I was no longer interested in what she had to say on the subject. I was beginning to think that other things might be equally, if not more, important.

"I think we should talk, Eve."

"We are talking, sweetie."

"No. You were talking, and I was happily not listening, but now I want to talk with you and have a conversation; a proper one."

"Okay, big boy, what about?"

I looked for somewhere to start. I was finding it difficult and instinctively picked on the least sensitive of the issues now crawling around my cranium as my starter for ten. "Why do you have all those books about Abel downstairs?"

Eve looked stupefied, as if the question was unexpectedly left field, which, all things being equal at that time, it probably was.

"What? Sorry?" Eve maintained an air of bafflement.

"The books in the library." I paused. "Do you even know what I am talking about? This is meant to be your house and your library. Do you even know what 'your family' book collection contains?"

"What are you on about?" Eve's tone was now getting as short as mine had become. "Of course, I know what's in my own library. I assume you're talking about the collection of the Books of Abel that's downstairs?" I nodded. "Somebody in the family started the collection and others followed. So what? Is this really necessary right now?"

"So why have you never mentioned them to me?"

Eve managed to look bemused and irritated in equal measure. "Part of me would like to say why should I, but if you would care to utilise that thing in your head for a moment — you know, that lump of soggy grey tissue that other people use as a brain — you might remember that I have previously suggested you explore the library and have a look at the collection because you might enjoy it. I thought it would amuse you to come across quite so many books with your name on them. So, maybe I have an odd sense of humour, so still — so what?"

Eve was clearly annoyed by my questioning. Was it the subject that was the problem or just my way of asking questions? I hadn't meant to make such a big thing over the books: Lily maybe, but not the books. Things hadn't gone according to plan, and I was starting to feel slightly chastened and cooler in my own agitation.

"Do I gather that you didn't find the books amusing?" There was now a definite note of sarcasm in Eve's voice.

"It was just a surprise to come across the books without warning or explanation. I thought you would have mentioned them in passing, given the coincidence of my name."

"You've already said that once and, by the way, you are wrong. The name 'Abel' is not a coincidence." It was my turn to look baffled, but Eve ploughed on, "Abel is a family name. At least one boy in every generation is given the name Abel. That's probably why someone started the collection in the first place. Perhaps my sense of humour is down to the family genes. Who knows? Anyway, when you told me that your true name was Abel, I felt certain you were part of the family. I was going to tell you once you had found the books, but that was the day I had to leave suddenly, and I never got the chance."

She paused, but I couldn't think of anything to say other than "Oh," and that sounded lame.

Eve's tone of voice mellowed, and she snuggled up to me again, rubbing flesh against flesh. "I didn't want to go and leave you, Abel, not so soon, but I didn't have a choice and then communication became difficult. You seemed upset, and I couldn't work out why. You only ever wanted to text me, and your messages were all so curt, that I decided it was best to wait until I could talk to you properly, face to face, body to body, and see how things were between us before I told you what I had found out."

"How things were between us? But we're okay now, aren't we?" I was suddenly, unexpectedly anxious. "You're back, and everything's good again, isn't it?"

Eve stroked my face gently and kissed my eyes shut: four sweet kisses, two per eye.

"Yes, we're okay, Abel, were okay, are okay, always okay. But, I do have to tell you what I've been looking into. I've found things out about our family, about you, and I'm afraid some of those things aren't okay, but you need to hear about them."

She had said "*our* family." She'd said that we'd always be okay. That was all I needed to know. I couldn't think of anything she could now come up with that would worry me.

"So tell me," I said. "Whatever you think you've found out, just tell me. It can't be that bad."

"Okay. If you're sure you're up for it. Here's the thing. Because you look the way you do, and because you told me you were named Abel, I felt sure that you must be family, but I needed to check you out, to be on the safe side, you know? While I was away, I asked around to find out who in the family was living where, who has children, who might have had children back in the sixties, and if any were boys called Abel. I got lucky. The woman I think was your mother was living in London towards the late sixties, which puts her in the right place at the right time. She was known as Lily then. She had a very brief relationship, which resulted in a baby, but she already had a little boy from a previous lover. He, the first son, had problems, and she didn't feel able to cope with another baby, so she gave away the second child. She did, however, make sure he was called Abel. Maybe she thought she'd be able to track him down once he had grown older? Things, however, didn't work out that way. The first boy wasn't totally well, and it took all her energy to look after him. She never had the opportunity to maintain contact with the second baby. She lost track of him, and then it was too late."

"Too late?"

"Lily has gone. I'm sorry."

Just like that: an end to my dreams. Another candle snuffed out. Not surprisingly, my face must have reflected this sudden darkness, let alone the background chorus of my thoughts, stunned by the volume of information that was flooding towards me after a lifetime of drought. Eve kept going, trying to bring me some good news.

"But the oldest boy is still alive. So, on the plus side you could still have some close family out there, but, on the other hand, that would be rather complicated if you really are the second son."

"Complicated? What do you mean by complicated?"

"As I said, the oldest boy wasn't at all well. Physically, he was extremely healthy, but he wasn't exactly stable. He could become violent and aggressive and was prone to mood swings. At times, his behaviour could be extreme and become a risk to himself and others. He needed firm handling and control. Lily was successful in providing that, and they established an extremely close relationship. Too close, probably, but it meant that he survived to grow up into an adult. That however, could give us a problem. Your brother is still alive and well, at least physically. Over the years, his potential for violence has apparently gotten worse and he has developed a jealous obsession with your mother. At one stage, he was living abroad, safely and with relatively few problems. The family had become involved and had made sure there were people to watch over him. He can be charming and his carers became too casual about their role. He got away from them. He was an adult. He had never actually been officially diagnosed or formally treated. The family looked into it, but there was nothing really that could be done, and at the time, they didn't think he would be a serious danger to anyone."

I was struggling to make sense of all of this. There was too much information, too quickly. It all seemed terribly unreal and melodramatic, like episodes from an overwritten soap opera. But, each new fact was stirring up real emotions in me that I hadn't expected and didn't feel capable of dealing with. I was in the eye of a huge storm, and my life was spinning away from me into the wildest part of the wind. I had only just got Eve back, everything was supposed to be good again, but then suddenly, it wasn't. I had been given a family at last: a mother and an unexpected brother, but then Lily, my mother (and how wonderfully and appropriately strange was that?), was gone, and my brother turned out to be a violent raving (uncertified) lunatic on the run from his minders. What was I supposed to make of this? What exactly should I be feeling?

"My father, you haven't mentioned my father. Who is he? Is he still alive?"

"It was a very brief relationship. The only close family I can tell you about is your brother."

"That would be the one with a possessive obsession with our mother and who is out there, somewhere, without restraint or minders? By the way, do you know which country he is now at large in? Just thought I'd ask."

Eve hesitated. "That's part of the problem. The last time anyone saw him, he was here in Britain. But there's more. He knows about you, and I'm not convinced that he's dreadfully happy to find out he has a long lost brother with whom he has to share his mother, so to speak."

"So, how does he know about me when I have only just now heard about him?"

Eve looked extremely uncomfortable. "I told him."

My life had run through the storm, found a high cliff on which to pause dramatically and was now about to fall off.

"You told him?"

"Yes. Only, I didn't know he was your brother then or anything about his history. He was just a relative. He was charming and very pleasant," Eve giggled disconcertingly. "And I had a chat with him about things."

The giggle was strange and seemingly inappropriate. I blanked any potential reason for the giggle. "You spoke to him on the phone?"

"No, I met him."

"In Britain, in person, which is why you know he's here."

"Yes."

"So, let me get this right: you have already met my unhinged and potentially violent brother who is currently at loose in the U.K. You, without knowing he was my brother, told him all about this family waif and stray you had picked up, namely me, and in so doing, gave him enough information for him to be able to identify me as his mother's previously unknown second son. He, having spent his life thinking he was an only child, therefore, and without any warning, found out that he was obliged to share his beloved mother, of whom he was already obsessively jealous, with someone else; a discovery he did not take kindly to. How am I doing?"

"Pretty spot on," Eve said.

"So, what did he say in response to the news of my existence?"

"Not a lot. He became rather agitated and wanted to ask me questions about you, rather than answer any of the questions I was trying to ask him. I started to feel uncomfortable and didn't tell him so much after that. So the conversation ground to something of a halt."

"So what, precisely, did you tell him about me?"

"As I said, not much, I didn't know that much myself at the time, but apparently it was enough for him to identify you and to know that you are alive and… and living here in London, and that you and I are together."

"Does he know where you live?"

"Yes." Things just carried on getting betterer and betterer.

"Okay, seeing as how you have told my brother about me, why don't you tell me something about my brother? What does he look like? How old is he? I know, let's start with his name."

"Cain."

Fate was clearly having a laugh.

XV

After further emotionally draining, but totally circular, discussions, from which I gleaned little more than I already knew, I returned to my own place that evening. It was a very big wrench leaving Eve, but after the emotional buffeting of the day, I needed the time and space to think and, as much as it hurt me to admit it, I thought better without Eve around. I could at least see that now. I was so infatuated with her and distracted by her physical presence, that I found it all too easy to lose my train of thought when she was close by. I also realised that I was starting to forget things altogether. So much new information had been thrown at me, so quickly, that I felt I needed time out. I needed to absorb facts, not forget them. It was going to take time to shape those facts and construct a sensible story around them and then, having done that, maybe I would know how I was supposed to feel.

The day had just been too much. Eve's return home, of itself, would have had more than enough emotional weight for me in my current state, without adding the confirmation that, after half a lifetime's wait, I had a family out there; that I was not alone any more. Fate was not satisfied, however, and had piled on the discovery that I had an unexpected brother, albeit a mentally suspect one, now, on the loose, and none too pleased with my existence; I pass over any irony our biblical nomenclature added to the situation. My visit to the house prior to Eve's return had also been stressful, and for the life of me, I could no longer remember why I had thought that playing at being a stalker was a good idea or what I'd hope to get from it, other than an excess of adrenaline that had paved the way for a full overdose later that afternoon. If I was honest with myself,

I had this nagging feeling there were still things to be resolved from my intrusion, but I wasn't going to give into it and allow myself to become distracted again. Eve was back, and I needed to concentrate on her and the news she had brought with her.

There was also the family to think about: *our* family. I now had a family, and that family had Eve in it. I assumed we were distant cousins of some sort. I couldn't now remember what relationship Eve had said we were to one another, but I wasn't that bothered. It wasn't too close for comfort or Eve would have said, and therefore the familial links just added to our personal bond.

With the exception of my mad and bad brother, all the news I had received was good, and how mad or bad could he be? Cain had never been sectioned or institutionalised. He had never actually harmed anyone, as far as I could tell. Eve had said there was a charming side to him, and though he had given his carers the slip, the family had seemingly just shrugged its collective shoulders and resigned itself to the fact that there was nothing to be done, so there couldn't have been that much of a risk. Wealthy families have, up until only relatively recently, been known for being overly sensitive about such things. They have locked away their own flesh and blood for the sin of merely being different; a "sin" that would have been protected, cosseted, and loved by many poorer, lower-class families. Perhaps Cain was the victim, not the bad guy.

I saw no reason to be anxious, other than Eve herself appeared to be. She had kept returning to the worry of Cain throughout the afternoon and had finally packed me off home with strict instructions to be on my guard and look out for him. Not that he was likely to be lurking nearby, or that I even knew what he actually looked like. Eve had attempted to describe him, but her description was so nebulous — tallish, late thirties/early forties, reasonably slim, reasonably good looking, dark hair, dark eyes — that she could have been describing me. I concluded that I needed clearer, more specific information about Cain. Tomorrow, I would need to press Eve for more, or at least better, detail.

In the meantime, there had been some sweet news to cling on to. This was the discovery that I so desperately wanted to spend time alone just savouring: Eve's confirmation that the photograph I had cherished all my life as of my mother was indeed of her. My mother; she had become real at last. The fact she was called Lily was even more amazing. That name had always had a resonance for me. Perhaps somehow, I knew. It was all an incredible coincidence. Somewhere at the back of my mind was an escaping memory of a painting of another woman called Lily, but I decided not to pursue it. I had more than enough on my plate just now, and I really needed to focus.

I was aware I needed to capture all of these thoughts and impressions in writing before they started to alter or I started to forget. By putting it all down in black and white, I could start the process of making sense of it. When Eve and I next talked about the family I'd take notes, which would help. In the meantime, I needed to do something to calm the gale force winds still swirling around my head and blowing my emotions all over the place. Otherwise, I was in danger of heading into the near perfect storm I sensed was brewing, and the words, like my emotions, were at risk of getting scattered and badly lost, maybe irrevocably.

In my book, the word is where things always begin, have always begun; is how things are envisaged and shaped. Writing things down, shaping and manipulating them, would return me to my origins and put me back in control.

I wondered how my brother (now there was a term that would take some getting used to) was dealing with the emotions generated by his discovery of me. Would he sit back and reflect, or would he seize the moment? Just how upset by these revelations was he? I felt I could empathise. He'd had years of certainty and sole possession, now taken away when, belatedly, he'd found he had to share. After years of uncertainty, I now had a mother, but she was no longer just mine, she was also Cain's. I was struggling with the thought of sharing my mother with anyone, even a brother, but I decided it was best not to go there; better to lose myself for a while in the promised sanctuary of the written word and capture my reflections on the day before the still sunlit images faded back into the dark.

XVI

I arranged to see Eve the following evening. In the meantime, I had a day-to-day life to maintain and a living to earn.

There had been a spate of shoplifting from the local shops. Nothing new in London, perhaps, but a gang of young children was suspected, a latter day Fagin's crèche, and therefore it was probably going to be worthy of an article or two in the local rag. My job this morning was to interview the afflicted shopkeepers, hopefully pick up some decent quotations, and then do a vox pop with other shop owners in the area and the local shopping population at large; the general theme being worry and irritation on the streets of North London. I wasn't really in the right frame of mind for the assignment, as my thoughts, rather than being focussed on the job in hand, were still obsessing about the news of the afternoon before or were racing ahead in anticipation of the forthcoming evening. I resented the interruption of work, but I needed to keep up the payments on my mortgage.

By the time I hit the High Road, I was already irritable and on edge, and that was before the first of my appointments. My irritation grew when I discovered that my first interviewee thought he was meeting me that afternoon, and was, therefore, unavailable for comment this morning. The spotty youth slouching over the cash till in his absence was not a suitable interview replacement, as "Yeah, wha'ever," in response to each and every question I asked was not going to make it into the top ten of insightful quotations of the week.

My second scheduled interview was even more frustrating, as the elderly lady who owned the local greengrocers was obviously several oranges short of a fruit basket. She kept insisting she had already spoken to me earlier on in the day and wasn't going to answer any more inappropriate questions. I could only hope my third interviewee was going to be more helpful. I had some time to kill before my final appointment, so I used it to speak to shoppers at random and to shopkeepers who had not yet experienced the supposed plague of kindergarten criminality. One of the latter suggested that some of the gang might even now be about their dirty deeds in the area, so in the interest of cutting-edge investigative journalism, I decided to keep my eyes open whilst wandering aimlessly up and down the High Road.

In the process, I spotted a likely candidate for the role of the Artful Dodger, a scruffy child of about nine or ten, who clearly should have been at school at this time of day, hanging around the local Budgens. When he went into the store, I kept an eye on him through the plate glass window at the front of the shop, which as a surveillance method seemed to work reasonably well until I noticed the reflection of someone staring as intently at me as I was at young Artful. I turned round to challenge him and if necessary explain that I was a journalist on the side of good, not an evil paedophile checking out small boys in the local supermarket, but there was no one there. I turned back to the window to resume surveillance of my potential criminal mastermind in the making, only to find that he had done a bunk. My irritation levels rose still further.

I wandered a bit further up the High Road, continuing to seek random opinions from random people whilst keeping my eyes open for the Artful Dodger or any other suspicious infants. To this end, I was peering in the window of another shop, this time a newsagent, when I saw the reflection of someone standing directly behind me, conveniently positioned to do little else but pick my pocket or indecently assault me. Neither was an attractive proposition. From his outline, it looked like a man of about my own height and build, but as I turned towards him, I almost fell over a little old lady and her shopping bag on wheels, which she had managed to position directly beside me. By the time the trolley had been righted and apologies had been exchanged, the owner of the reflection had gone.

A few shops further down the road were a joke and fancy dress shop, and there were a couple of young candidates for the Borough Youth

Offending Team's ministrations hanging around the doorway. When they went inside, I took up a position beside the door and in front of the shop window. I was partially watching them and simultaneously looking out for anyone who appeared to be watching me. I wasn't exactly successful on either score. I always had the feeling that I was missing out in terms of the direction I wasn't looking. Whilst turning my head like an owl in search of mice, I startled myself with my own reflection in the glass. It was dark and distorted, deep in the glass, and brought back the memory of the marred image I had seen in the cabinet door in Eve's library. This gave me an unpleasant jolt and a feeling that I was missing something important. When I repositioned my head, I lost the image and then couldn't get it back. Finally, I saw the demon mask in the window, roughly where I had first caught sight of my reflection, its third eye positioned in its forehead, directly between its eyebrows. What was wrong with my sense of self image these days? It was as if I had become unable to recognise myself. Fortunately, there was no one around to witness my embarrassment. By the time I had got my act together, the two youngsters had left the shop. So much for my undercover reporting skills. My head was so not where it needed to be. I was becoming increasingly distracted and jumpy, and, in turn, irritated at myself for being so plain stupid.

I decided I was so wired that a strong black coffee couldn't make matters any worse, but might serve to make me warmer and give me an excuse to sit down for a bit. I abandoned the ill-fitting role of super sleuth journalist and went inside the little Italian café on the corner. The coffee was good, as was the jam doughnut I ate to counteract the coffee's wetness.

Having drunk my coffee and two more for luck, I needed to undrink all the liquid I had just consumed before going back out into the big, bad, and rather chilly world. I still had to do my final interview before returning to the office to attempt to make silken prose out of the pig swill of comments I had collected so far. There was a small toilet at the back of the café, and as I headed there, I heard the next customer come into the café behind me; two customers in under an hour, business was booming in this neck of the woods.

Nature having been attended to, I was washing my hands in the none too clean basin — optimism wins out every time — when I glanced up at myself in the mirror over the sink and did a double take, literally. I could see two of me. For a split second, I thought either my eyesight was in urgent need of a trip to the optician's or the mirror was defective. Then my brain and my eyes got it together and confirmed normal service. There were two reflections in the mirror because there were two people standing in front of it. A tall, dark-haired man was standing behind me and looking at my reflection looking at him. I turned round as quickly as possible in the less than generous space available and stared straight, to all intents and purposes, into my own face. The only difference was the faint scarring on the man's forehead between his eyebrows. The face smiled broadly at me, revealing teeth far whiter and straighter than mine; clearly someone who had not been subject to the ministrations of an NHS dentist in the early seventies.

The owner of the face spoke, "Hello brother. I think we need to talk."

His name was Cain. He did not come across as raving or psychotic. He was my brother, and I was surprised to find that he was a part of me that had always been there. I just hadn't realised it before. Talking to Cain was as natural as talking to myself.

Physically, there was little to differentiate us. Cain was, maybe, one or two inches taller than me, slightly broader across the shoulders, and clearly fitter, the benefits of a private income and a private trainer. The only other really obvious differences were the teeth, the private income again, and maybe the scarring on the forehead, although in the current lighting, it was barely noticeable.

Our histories, however, couldn't have been further apart. I told him of the joys of local government-funded social care. He told stories about the life of a young prince: money no object, and surrounded by servants focussed entirely on his needs. If there was an element of a gilded cage to his experiences, the bars dazzled so brightly that they concealed it.

Yet, despite this gulf between our two disparate backgrounds, there were more similarities than differences. I watched him as he talked and saw my own physical mannerisms re-enacted. I listened to him speak and heard the echo of my voice. I absorbed his stories and detected my own way of looking at the world. I was no longer alone. Blood had created something that was part of me, but beyond me, something that I was part of and belonged to. This was a lifetime's dreaming suddenly come true, and I wanted to savour it. During our first hours together, I felt no fear of Cain. Indeed, I was so comfortable with him that I was able to lean back into a feeling of familial warmth and ease in much the same way you lean back into a warm bath after a hard day's physical labour.

But, even a good bath eventually gets cold, and as time progressed, I felt a growing sense of both irritation and disquiet. I had had almost forty years of living with myself as a creature of fixed boundaries and borders. I was singular and unfathomable, even to myself, and now this brother had come along and casually started to behave as though he knew me. To make matters worse, it almost seemed as if he did. The more I studied him, the more I saw aspects of myself I had always assumed were mine alone. I had wanted a family because I had wanted something that was mine, unique to me. But, now I had it, I had lost my uniqueness, and I wasn't sure I was entirely comfortable with this. Being with Cain was like being with myself, but my personal borders were becoming less clear cut as a result. It was those tightly guarded borders that had kept the dark places separate and me sane all these years. No, I wasn't comfortable at all.

There was another reason for my growing discomfort and that was solely down to Eve. Her words of warning about Cain were echoing in my head as I listened to his stories and became increasingly aware that those stories did not exactly fit with Eve's take on events. Sure, Eve had confirmed that when Cain grew older the family had provided him with a gilded cage for his own welfare and the safety of others, but Eve's story of my mother's earlier struggles as a single parent, just about coping to bring Cain up and keep him on the straight and narrow, whilst too poor and too desperate to care for me as well, did not feature in Cain's narrative of gold-plated luxury in the expensive watering holes of affluent Europe. Either Eve had got her facts seriously wrong, or Cain had only a limited acquaintance with the concept of reality.

After our initial meeting in the private facilities of the café, we had walked across the road to the nearest pub and had been sharing our past lives over, in my case, a much-needed pint or two and, for Cain, several Jack Daniels on the rocks. I was conscious of Eve's warnings about the explosive potential to Cain's personality, despite the currently charming exterior, but the differences between Eve's take on things and Cain's recollections were increasing, and I felt that I could no longer simply ignore this. It would somehow be letting Eve down if I didn't challenge Cain's viewpoint. I shied away from direct confrontation, however, and approached the matter obliquely and from a reasonable distance. First, I introduced Eve edgeways into the conversation and was surprised by the nature of the response.

"I shall have to thank Eve for helping you track me down."

Cain looked momentarily taken aback by my comment, but then quickly regained his composure. "Yes, I guess you could say that." Cain's statement sounded more like a question.

"I mean, if you and Eve hadn't met up recently, I guess you wouldn't have known about me."

"Oh, I have always known about you, little brother. I just didn't know where to find you." I wasn't sure what to make of that, but whatever Cain meant by it, it didn't seem to match Eve's version of events.

"Eve has told me you didn't know you had a half brother until she raised the matter with you."

"No. I have always been aware of your existence. Eve hinted it was the right time to come and find you, but I hadn't realised you were not aware of me until only just now."

It was my turn to be taken aback. My comfort levels were slipping once more. This wasn't what Eve had told me. What sort of game was Cain playing?

Cain seemed to read my discomfort. "Abel, I haven't come to you with subtle games. That's not my way, anymore than it is yours. It is, however, Eve's way and from what you have been saying, I don't think she has dealt you a straight hand. There is a good deal that you clearly haven't been told, but I don't know why, and I don't think it's my business to tell you at this present time."

"What do you mean? What is it that I don't know and why won't you tell me?"

"I am not my brother's keeper. You need to speak to the one who thinks she is." He downed the rest of his drink and stood up. "I've got to tell you, brother, I am not good at keeping secrets. That's where you and I differ. If we keep on talking like this, I'll end up telling you something you need to hear from someone else. I am sorry, I was too eager to see you. If I had realised that things were like this, I would have stayed away for a while longer." He started towards the door.

"Wait," I stood up too. "You can't go all cryptic on me and then walk out without an explanation. What are you talking about? What is it that I need to know?"

Cain looked torn and very keen to be out the door. "Look, how aware of our mother are you? Have you seen any of the paintings of Lily yet?"

"Paintings of our mother? All I have of her is the photograph she left with me. I don't know anything about paintings of her. I've certainly never seen one."

"Haven't you?" And as he said that, an image of my mother's photograph overlaid the picture of a woman in a midnight blue velvet dress. A painting of Lily, stashed away in Eve's house and repeatedly denied by her; a painting which had meant so much to me, yet which, somehow, I had never managed to challenge her over; a painting which I had almost managed to forget, yet again. Perhaps it wasn't just Cain who had defective mental wiring.

Cain stood and watched me whilst I wrestled with things in my head. As soon as he had decided that I had won the match, he turned round and walked out of the door with a thoughtful "Au revoir."

My thoughts were persistently determined, however, to have a rematch with themselves. They carried on struggling with their own sensed contradictions well after he had gone. Someone clearly was not at home in the realms of truth and reality, but whether that someone was Cain, Eve, or me, I was starting to have trouble telling.

XVII

I was so shaken up by the unexpected conclusion of my meeting with Cain and the thoughts it had churned up from the long accumulated silt at the bottom of my skull that I couldn't last out to the evening to speak to Eve. As soon as I got back to the relative stability of home, I phoned her. She answered immediately and seemed extremely alarmed to hear I had met up with my brother.

"Be careful, Abel. Promise me you'll be careful. Cain is a complex man. He is not to be trusted, and he could be a danger to you. I don't want you getting hurt."

"He was fine," I reassured her. "On the whole, we got on amazingly well and things were all very pleasant and civilised. There was never any suggestion that he was going to thump me. Besides, in the middle of the lounge bar of The Bald Faced Stag, what's he going to do?"

"I don't know. I just want you to be careful and stay on your guard."

"Look, Cain was fine. In many ways it seemed like a very natural coming together. The pieces of the jigsaw fitted, and Cain couldn't have been friendlier. It was only at the end that things got a bit strange."

Eve leapt on that comment. "Strange? How strange? What did he do? I told you that you needed to be careful."

"He didn't do anything. It was just what he said. He got rather cryptic at the end and implied there were things I didn't know about that I needed to. I think he's seen the painting of Lily, you know the one you say you've never seen?"

"As I keep saying, I haven't seen it."

"Well, I think he has, and he implied that in some way it's connected to our mother."

"That's really worrying. You can't trust him, Abel. What exactly did he say?"

I realised I was on awkward ground. How could I respond to this interrogation without sounding like the village idiot? Was I really going to say that he had simply asked a question, and I had immediately jumped to conclusions by recalling a painting I had apparently forgotten for the moment, despite being obsessed with it for years, and linking it to my mother? Our mother. Plus, there was Eve's repeated denial of the painting to take into account. A permutation of the truth, rather than the actual truth, seemed like a good idea. I took a flyer.

"He asked me if I had seen the paintings of Lily that you keep at the house."

There was a long pause at the other end of the phone.

"Abel, you've been here. You've seen the paintings on the walls. There are no paintings of Lily." I could see the light at the back of a dark cupboard: my dark, secret, illuminated love. I couldn't believe that Eve was still brazenly lying about this.

"What about the painting in the cupboard?"

"What cupboard would that be?"

"The one in the Drawing Room. It's pointless pussy-footing about anymore, Eve. I have seen the painting of Lily in there. In the cupboard. In the Drawing Room. In your house."

"Okay, Abel, Okay. If you say so. Let's not fight over this. When you come over tonight, we will look in the cupboard together and see what is in there. Then we'll talk some more." She hung up on me then, slowly.

When I arrived at the house that evening, Eve seemed more concerned than passionate.

"How are you feeling?"

"I'm fine. I got a bit agitated when we were talking, but now I'm fine. I just don't understand all the secrecy and denial over a painting."

"No secrecy, Abel. No denial. I've been telling you the truth. If you don't believe me come and see for yourself."

She led me through into the Drawing Room. The cupboard door was shut and almost invisible in the subdued glow of the low level, table lamp lighting. Eve stood beside the door and opened it. Waiting in the interior gloom was a small step ladder, a bucket, and a mop. At the back of the cupboard hung an old and stained dark blue velvet curtain. I reached in and pulled the curtain back, revealing a wall covered in browned and faded wallpaper with a pattern of willow leaves; the remains of a much earlier phase of the house's interior décor. There was no painting.

"Where is it?" I demanded.

"Where is what?"

"The painting. The painting of Lily. You know what I mean; there is no need to carry on playing games."

"Abel, I am not the one playing games. I do not have the painting, and if I did, I am sure I wouldn't choose to keep it in a dingy cleaning cupboard."

"But I've seen it here, twice now, and Cain reminded me of that."

Eve seized on the mention of my brother with vehemence. "Cain? Cain? What has he got to do with it? I keep warning you about him. He's not to be trusted. He's not a well man. But he's clever, and if he sees any similar weakness in you, he'll use it. Be honest, now, why would you need Cain to remind you of a painting that, by your own admission, you have been fascinated with for years?"

I didn't want to go there. Explaining the reasons for my repeated absent-mindedness over the painting was a difficult one. I didn't understand it. If I couldn't convince myself, how was I going to convince Eve?

"I didn't need him to remind me. He just did." Not the most erudite response, but a whole lot better than the truth.

Eve took a gentle but audible breath. "Abel, tell me what Lily, the woman in the painting, is wearing."

"A long dress. A long, midnight blue velvet, dress."

"Midnight blue velvet, like the colour of this curtain material?"

"Yes"

The suggestion that I might be sufficiently confused to mistake a length of old curtain for an eighteenth century portrait hung unsaid between us. Could I have been that obsessed that I had imagined seeing the painting? Did more than a physical likeness run in Cain's and my DNA?

"Come and have a drink, and let's forget about this for this evening." Eve moved over to the coffee table where a bottle of La Luna's dark red had already been opened and filled two glasses. I downed mine in one go and poured myself another one. "Families are complicated. Damaging games get played. You've never really had one, so you wouldn't know. Cain is a game player. He's sick, but he's clever. He'll twist your thoughts. You must keep away from him. He could be dangerous. He isn't to be trusted, especially not by you. I want you safe. Promise me you will take care and stay away from him. Promise me."

I promised, of course. What else could I do?

We ate in that night. Unseen hands had already set the table in the dining room and lit row after row of candles, arranged for effect around the room. The food was as good as that served at La Luna. If the conversation was still a little stilted at the start of the meal, a second bottle of wine put paid to that and things seemed to be returning to normal. We talked about everything other than the things that really mattered, but that seemed normal, too. And the most normal thing of all, despite the fiasco at the start of the evening, was for both of us to end up in Eve's bed in a cacophony of snowy sheets, night black hair and the all pervading scent of lilies.

XVIII

Several days passed before I saw Cain again. I spent them at work or with Eve. My thoughts remained confused, but thankfully, I had little time for introspection or, when I was with Eve, for thinking at all. I lost myself in her. I liked it that way. Towards the end of the week, however, Eve told me she had other evening commitments, and so I made my solitary way back to my own flat for once. I had plans to use the downtime constructively. I felt I needed to write, to use the available space to shape my words in the hope that I could sort out some of my feelings by spilling them across the non-judgemental blank of a sheet of paper, or at least fix them on the blankness so that they would remain in one place.

Cain was standing, waiting for me, by my front door. He was quite open about it; the combined illumination of London's street lights and the liquid silver of the night's full moon left little room for shadows to lurk or be lurked in. Somewhere up in the heavens, the stars were wasting their energy by shining both virtuously and vigorously, but it was far too bright to see the benefits of their efforts. I knew that I wasn't scared of Cain, but I was prepared to admit to not feeling completely safe with him, either. Eve's repeated warnings had done the trick. I was saved from the dilemma of deciding whether or not to ask him in by his making it very clear that this was only a fleeting visit.

"I'm not supposed to be here, so we'd better make this quick. I can guess what she's told you, but you are as ill-advised to trust her as she has no doubt said you are to trust me. The easiest way is not to believe either of us. Believe yourself, Abel. That's the only way forward."

I wanted to tell him that I was beginning to recognise it was fast becoming the weakest of all the options open to me, but I thought better of it. Cain was looking very agitated and intense. The white light of the moon was not doing him any favours. His skin looked deathly white, and the slight furrows in his face were made to look like deep gullies. The scarring on his forehead looked like a brand. It was so marked that I was surprised at not having paid it that much attention before. In summary, he looked like the sort of man you wouldn't want to meet all alone in a gloomy front garden at night. I tried to edge away discreetly, but he grabbed my arm and pulled me firmly towards him. For the first time I started to have real doubts about my safety.

"Stay here in the moonlight; it's safer that way, particularly tonight, when the bright moon is at full strength. The darker one is forced to stay hidden." The definition of the word "lunatic" passed slowly across the inside of my brain. I maintained a tactful silence, but prudently stayed in the light. "There are things you need to know about me, little brother; things about our loving family and about yourself. Eve should have told you, but, as ever, she's playing a convoluted game of her own. It's not my place to tell you what she won't. And even if I could, you wouldn't believe me." His judgement was spot on there. "As you won't trust me and mustn't trust Eve, you will have to find out for yourself. You were always the one for words. I just hope that reading the truth will help you see things for what they are. Eve has told me that she has hidden all the paintings, with the exception of one still exhibited in a gallery. I guess you will know which one that is. However, I don't think she has removed the books from the library yet. They're yours, really, the ones in the glass cabinet. You need to read them, soon, whilst there is still time to do so. It's your story, and you need to reclaim it. You need to believe and understand it before you can write it."

I didn't know how to respond. Cain wasn't exactly frothing at the mouth, but he was clearly raving. Eve's words of warning came back to me with a vengeance. I didn't want to say anything to antagonise him, but I didn't want to encourage him either. I decided that repetition was the better part of valour. "I need to believe it before I can write it."

"Yes." He seemed to be waiting for more from me.

"I need to read the books in the cabinet." I paused. "The books in the cabinet are the ones I need to read."

Echoes of a Danny Kaye film I remembered seeing as a child played in my head, and I resisted the urge to start reciting rhyming couplets. Cain clearly could not see the humour of it all.

"Yes, you do. And soon. The word is where it began and always now begins; for you, at least. You need to read before you can write, and understand before you can choose. If you don't believe the first book you read, read another one, and then another. Read the whole fucking lot of them if necessary; just read them. They'll all tell you the same thing: the truth. They'll tell you who you are and what you are. Promise me you'll read them. Promise." I promised. I was getting quite good at making promises. It was keeping them that gave me difficulty.

"I can't stay here. I need to go while the moon is still high," said Cain and lunged at me. I was too slow, and he grabbed me, pinioning my arms to my sides and squeezing the air out of my lungs. For a brief moment we were face to face, all personal space abandoned, two halves of the same disconcerting reflection. I was genuinely terrified. Then he kissed me vigorously on both cheeks and ran off up the road, keeping to the well illuminated parts of the street.

I let myself into my flat and quickly polished off a couple of stiff whiskies. Eve was right, families were complicated. Cain had convinced me he was a raving lunatic and had scared me shitless in the process, but there was something raw in that final frenzied hug that had reached out to me. It had felt like love, whatever that was, and if he loved me, he wasn't going to hurt me, right? He was clearly as barking as a Chihuahua in an over-stuffed handbag, but he was my brother, and I had never had one of those before, however uncomfortable it sometimes felt. Despite the incipient madness, I identified with him. It was as if there were two of me now, and both were in need of a little understanding. I decided I was going to read the books as promised, not in the expectation of finding out the truth, because it was unlikely to be hiding itself in musty, yellowing pages, and who knows what it is anyway, but because I hoped it might help me understand Cain a little better and provide me with an appropriate response the next time we met or he freaked out on me again.

XIX

The only time is the present, whichever way you choose to look at it. I decided I would check out the collected Books of Abel the following day. The fact that Eve was still away from home was an added incentive to go for the here-and-now. It wasn't that I didn't want Eve to know what I was doing, it was just that I thought it would be easier if she didn't; less complicated, fewer explanations required. I have never really liked explaining. It seems to require a level of introspection that I am not that comfortable with. And what happens when you look inside yourself and find nothing reflected back? I much prefer the art of reporting, where you only have to gather hard facts and shape them to fit your story without necessarily lying or looking into things too deeply. I commend journalism to you as a way of holding body, mind, and soul together.

As Eve was out and about, I could have free run of the library and its books for the whole morning. The household help maintained, as ever, their invisibility. My comings and goings seemed of little interest to them, as far as I could tell. This was my time to see if I could work out just what, if anything other than mental illness was eating my brother. One man's insanity is another's individuality and inspiration, when all's said and done.

I let myself in at the front door — somewhere along the way, I seemed to have acquired a key, although I couldn't exactly remember when or how, but it was an improvement on my previous method of clandestine ingress.

The household help had clearly been busy that morning. The hall was filled with the scent of fresh flowers. Three huge vases of full, blousy pink roses and assorted other paler flora occupied pride of place on the hall tables, but it was the scent of lilies that dominated the air. It was like walking into a fragrant garden. It wasn't just me that was confused by the sudden blossoming of nature within a townhouse. An industrious bee was attempting to visit each and every flower in turn. I wished it luck. It already seemed exhausted, drunk or drugged, and it had a long, lonely task ahead of it. I hope the hive appreciated its sacrifice.

I walked through the flower show and went straight to the library, only to find Eve seated at the desk. I felt a black wave of required explanations rolling towards me. It seemed, however, that luck was on my side this morning. Eve didn't look at all surprised and simply said, "Abel! Gosh that was quick. You can't have got my message much more than ten minutes ago."

It seemed like a good time to ignore the vibrations of the mobile phone in the depths of my inside jacket pocket, alerting me to the arrival of a new text message and fudge it. Always stick to the things you are best at, that's my motto.

"You call, I come," I said and performed a mock low bow. Eve smiled graciously, as if a minion responding to her summons in this way was only right and proper. I had a sudden feeling that in her case, it wasn't play acting. Or was I being overly sensitive? Her facial expression almost immediately shifted from enigmatically imperious to girlishly joyful.

"I've got such wonderful news that I'm glad I didn't have to wait long to tell you. I'm so happy, I just had to share it immediately." I naively assumed she had won the lottery or inherited another couple of million from an aged relative. I wasn't expecting what came next. "I'm pregnant. We're having a baby!"

This was not what I wanted to hear. I had progressed through my adult life to-date not wanting children. Hell, I had sacrificed more than one promising relationship to my avowed intent not to be a father. I didn't really know what a father was, but I didn't want to be one. I had problems enough with being a son and was struggling with being a brother. There was no way I wanted to be a daddy, but here was Eve laughing and crying, and forcing her way into my arms, whilst telling me that precisely that was to be my fate.

"Oh darling, isn't it wonderful? We're having a baby. I want it to be a little you. So sweet. I'll call him Abel. You'd like that wouldn't you? He's going to be us in perpetuity."

If Eve was getting ahead of herself, I didn't particularly notice at the time. I had gone into shock. Fatherhood had crept up on me unexpectedly and mugged me viciously, leaving me a traumatised victim. I wanted to scream all the usual mantras of avoidance such as "Are you sure? How do you know it's mine?" and of course "Why weren't you more careful? Didn't you have the sense to take precautions?" But somehow, I managed not to. I don't think I'm that much of a chauvinist, not really, but I had really thought she had things under control; she always seemed to have. I couldn't understand what had gone wrong or how she'd allowed this to happen.

Eve was still chattering away, suddenly turned girlish and giggly in a way I hadn't seen before or ever expected of her. I thought women were supposed to grow up and become maternal at the first signs of a little one's advent, but the opposite appeared to be happening to Eve. The giggling and inconsequential chattering showed no signs of slowing down. In her excitement she was almost skipping about and she was totally oblivious to my writhing discomfort, so wrapped up in the glittering and fluffy clouds of incipient motherhood that were wafting around her. She was still talking at me.

"That's okay, isn't it Abel? You don't mind doing it, do you?" I had no idea what it was she wanted me to do other than be a dad, and I wasn't in a fit state to answer that question. I wanted to howl like a wolf with its leg in a trap, but clearly couldn't do that and maintain any semblance of human dignity. Eve prattled on regardless. "Good, I'll go and get the camera." Just what had I agreed to do, and was it really necessary, given the imminent end of my world?

Eve returned quickly, clutching an expensive looking digital camera. "Let's take it here in the library." I remained nonplussed, and then suddenly, I wasn't anymore, although I desperately still wanted to be. Having thrust the camera into my hands, Eve strode towards the book cabinet devoted to my namesake, turned round and posed; the same position, limb perfect, as favoured by my mother and other female family members. I wanted to be sick. "Are you ready to take the picture?"

I moved on automatic, just like the camera, and somehow the photograph was taken. There, captured within the camera screen, like an illuminated portrait, was Eve, shadowed by the earlier Mrs. Striga, Lily, and my mother; a single woman, yet all four standing there, staring in unashamed maternal pride right back at the image taker. Their glance fixed and trapped me more permanently than I had captured their image.

Eve returned the book she had been holding in her hands to the cabinet and came forward to liberate both the camera and her secured picture from me.

"I just love the instant gratification of digital photographs," she said and smiled, not like a little girl any more, not even like my former lover, but more like a tiger seeing a small, helpless and deliciously plump lamb.

XX

The rest of that morning passed in a blur of disbelief and the queasiness of denial, but there was no getting away from it: I was about to become a father. However violently I wriggled, I remained on the hook, and the wriggling just served to tear away at me. Then, suddenly, it was the afternoon and, having been given leave to depart the presence, I was back in my flat, except who that "I" was, I was no longer quite so sure. Years of creating a self that I could live with, that I had expected to live with for the foreseeable future, were being undone in front of my eyes. If I looked in the mirror now, who would I see?

A small and dusty worker bee was wearing itself out, trying to batter its way to freedom through the glass in my window. With nothing better to do, I watched it for a while, but that just gave my negative thoughts the opportunity to multiply. They seized the opportunity with a vengeance. I needed a different form of distraction.

I had a stiff drink; I had several. The several multiplied. I just could not accept this was happening. I was losing Eve. She had been mine, but now there was going to be a baby with its own needs and demands. Eve was no longer mine and mine alone. She had willingly given herself away, but it wasn't just Eve I was losing. I was in danger of losing part of my identity, and it had taken so long to construct in the first place. In a few short weeks I had gone from being a motherless orphan to a man with a mother, a family, and a past I still didn't fully understand. I had gone from being an only child, to one of two, and the two so similar it seemed like looking into only a marginally distorted mirror. At times I even found myself doubting where one image ended and the other began. Now, I was doomed to be a father. What did that look like? I had another drink.

With hindsight, I realised things had started to crumble when I allowed myself to become lost in another person. Eve had taken me to places I hadn't known I'd wanted to go. I had abandoned myself completely in her, only to be exposed and betrayed. This woman had stolen part of me and used it to breed a child I was supposed to love, or something, and take responsibility for. How was I going to do that, when I had only barely coped with my own needs up until now? It seemed I was gradually dissolving into other people, losing myself to them. It wasn't a coincidence that my brother looked so much like me, and Eve talked of creating a little Abel. They were doppelgangers, stealing me away, bit by bit, and draining me of who I was.

Reality was duplicitous. Everything was being replicated, copied, doubled. The world had become filled with shadows all feeding off one another, feeding off me, and making me less than I was.

Eve had replicated my mother's photographic pose, taking away the one thing I had of my mother. I looked at the photograph of my mother now and saw an image of Eve overlaying it. Behind her, I could see Lily and Mrs. Striga, image overlaying image like eternally reflecting mirrors. When I looked at the postcard of Mrs. Striga's painting, I was confronted by the same multiple images of Lily, Eve, and my mother, and with them the shadows of nameless other women, all alike, all overlapping, no longer a single female, but a multitude. Where was the woman I had loved?

Where was my mother, who by rights should have belonged to me alone? But she hadn't, not truly, there had always been Cain before there had ever been me. I just hadn't known it. Cain with his face overlaying mine, soon to be joined by the little Abel that Eve was making. All my life I had been plagued by one little Abel. Would there now be two, or would I be supplanted by a child yet to be? Could the future Abel erase me from my own past, as Cain was seemingly managing to do? And what of that future? It was changing without my consent. Were the cracks of the past starting to make fissures into the future, or was the future clawing its way backwards into the past?

Was this a forewarning, or just the normal destruction of self and freedom that unwanted parenthood brings? So many questions, but where were the answers? How was I supposed to know?

I finished the bottle and looked for another drink. I was out of whisky, but at least I had a bottle of La Luna's special stashed away in the cupboard.

I now saw the books that Cain was pushing me to read as no more of a coincidence than Cain's looks or Eve's pregnancy; bookshelves of faceless Abels, each one over written by succeeding editions and authors. What did it feel like? Did the writers know they were just episodes in a centuries-long series, or had they lost themselves in a single man: multi-faceted, a hive mind, growing ever more and more complex as the pages filled with ink and the volumes spread out along the shelves?

The bee was continuing to beat itself to a noisy death against the window pane. My thoughts throbbed in time to its increasingly frantic efforts. As they pulsed they began to blossom and expand like fractals, taking me onward, taking me away. Wherever I was headed, rational thought was no longer accompanying me. It had proved to be just another aspect of my persona that had left me along the way, driven off by betrayal and a stifling fog of whisky and wine fumes. But for every subtraction I experienced, there were worrying additions.

Everything was continuing to multiply. Images overlaid images, which gave way to others, filling my vision like a swarm of agitated bees. And at the centre of the swarm was a queen, calm and unhurried, waiting, surveying the confusion through the multi-faceted filter of her eyes. I was lost to the swarm, but she knew where I was. She always knew. She was watching, and when I looked directly at her, all I could see was my own face reflected back at me in every part of her compound eyes, each as big as a single dark moon, and then I started falling.

XXI

Eventually, my head began to clear, but clarity would not be an accurate description of what I was left with. The swirling apidae were swallowed by a stagnant grey fog that penetrated everything. It doused my panic with inertia, filling every cubic inch of my skull with a solid aching absence. It took me over more effectively than the doppelgangers of my paranoia.

In due course, a spark of rational thought cleared a space for itself at the back of my head and attempted to burn off the fog, but what followed was not relief, just a sense of growing despair as the numbness retreated. Reality was inherently depressing in its own right. There was going to be a child, my child, and my life would be irrevocably changed. Whatever fathers were, I was becoming one.

I could not say how long I remained in this state. Nothing served to distract me from it. Sleep was my only escape, and so I slept. I surrendered my self to the comfort of oblivion until summoned back into the drab world of reality by a heavy knocking on my front door.

Eve was standing there, a large bouquet of roses and lilies in her arms; her gift to the sickly. The cloying scent of the flowers marched in ahead of her.

Eve was positively glowing. Wearing a heavily patterned dress of black and red roses, which clung to her still slim frame; motherhood suited her far more than fatherhood suited me. She was blooming, while I had developed the mental equivalent of morning sickness. Somehow, she had turned herself into Supermum in mothering overdrive. As soon as she got into the flat she started to fuss over the state it was in, as well as the state of me. I just let her. I had neither the energy nor the inclination to resist.

For someone whom I had only seen accustomed to being served and waited upon, she took to domesticity remarkably well. She found a vase for the flowers, along with my limited house cleaning equipment, and the flat was soon decluttered and cleansed. In the process, she came across the black and white photograph of my mother. I saw her pick it up and stare at it thoughtfully before resuming her one-woman clean up operation.

I was made to take a shower and change my clothes, and by the time I had re-emerged, the flat was miraculously pristine. Judging by her attitude towards me, Eve seemed to have been expecting that my showering would clean and invigorate the inside of my head as well as scrub me up physically. She was clearly disappointed that I was still as cerebrally shambolic as ever, but she attempted understanding and modulated her tone of voice accordingly. Needless to say, our conversation was decidedly stilted. She had sensitivity enough to avoid raising the issue of the baby directly, but from time to time I was sure I caught her rubbing her still-flat stomach with the satisfied smirk of a python digesting its lunch.

I was struggling to recall the exotic and intoxicating Eve who had so bewitched me such a short time ago. Where had she gone, or was it me who had left the building?

Eve tried to talk, but there were suddenly so many no-go areas that we were reduced to long periods of uncomfortable silence. In the pauses, I found my thoughts chasing after Cain and the peculiarities he had last exhibited. Were they any worse than mine? Who knew, but his were perplexingly of more interest to me. I wasn't sure why, but I found myself fretting over his parting words, repeating them silently, until they started to join in with the clammer being generated by the rest of the clutter in the dull cavity above my shoulders. I decided to initiate my own cerebral clean up operation in the hope of resolving at least one small thing and thereby starting to reduce the rusty junk stored in my cranium.

I raised the issue of the books with Eve. She seemed surprised and then irritated that I should still be bothering myself with such trifles when the rest of my life clearly needed significant sorting.

"Oh Abel, not again. What do you want to know about them for? They're old and dusty, just an old family eccentricity, nothing worth obsessing over."

"I was thinking about them, not obsessing. That's all. I thought they might be interesting to talk about. I mean, what are they actually about? Why collect so many copies of the same book. They are the same book, aren't they? It might be…"

"Look," Eve cut through my witterings, "I've told you before, they are just some family quirk. A stupid trifle that kept our granddaddies happy. Who'd have known, but obsessive behaviour seems to be another of the family traits."

"So, what were they obsessing about?"

"You tell me. Dry old stuff, theological claptrap. It was the reference to your name that I thought might amuse, not the contents of those dusty old tomes. It was just a stupid game on my part, and I don't feel like playing games anymore. Okay?"

"Have you actually read them?"

"Bits, here and there. They're hideously tedious."

"Has Cain ever read them?"

"Maybe. Quite possibly. You'd have to ask him, but I don't recommend it. You shouldn't go anywhere near him"

"Can I read them?"

"If you really want to, but not just now, eh? When you're feeling a bit better. They're not the stuff for convalescence."

There was one of those long uncomfortable pauses you usually only get at a bereavement. I stared at the floor where her handbag happened to be. There was a photograph sticking out of one of the side pockets and, without asking, I pulled it out. It was a colour print of the photo of Eve I had taken the other day.

"Why did you copy the pose in my mother's photo?"

"I posed like you asked. What photo is it like?"

"The photograph of my mother."

"Sorry?"

"What do you mean, 'Sorry?' I only have the one photo of her. So it's *the* photo. *The* photo you were looking at earlier. What fucking photo do you think I mean?"

"Okay, okay. There's no need to get agitated, Abel. I didn't want to upset you again. I hadn't realised you had a photo of her. Why don't you show it to me?"

I couldn't understand why she was lying so outrageously. Was this her idea of a joke? An appropriate game to play at a time like this? I went to the shelf where the photo was, but it wasn't there. I started to search through all the things on the shelf she had tidied up, untidying more and more vigorously in the process.

"What have you done with it? You were right, now is not the time for playing silly games."

"What have I done with what?" Eve sounded resigned rather than questioning.

"The photo. The one we were just talking about, remember? The one you were looking at before I had my shower."

"I'm sorry Abel. I really don't know what you're talking about. I came over because you hadn't phoned. I was worried about you. The last thing I wanted to do was upset you, but it seems I have. I think I'd better go now and come back when you're feeling a bit better. Give me a call tomorrow and let me know how things are." And with that, she picked up her handbag and headed straight for the door, not even a glance back over her shoulder. I yelled invectives at her retreating back, but made no attempt to stop her. She showed no sign of hearing me, anyway.

As soon as she had shut the front door, I tore the flat apart looking for the photo, but I couldn't find it. I had to assume it was no longer there. I had lost my mother once again, and this time I held Eve solely responsible.

XXII

I had loved Eve, I mean really loved Eve, but the days of long lunches floating on a sea of La Luna's dark red wine and nights cast adrift in billowing white sheets and entangling thick black hair were over.

Cain had known. He had tried to warn me. She plays games, he said, but I hadn't listened. Cain wasn't mad. He had the clearest vision of all of us, and that was why Eve was so scared of him. What else did he know about Eve? I needed to speak to Cain, but doing so wasn't going to be as easy as I hoped.

Cain knew where I lived and how to find me, but I now realised that I could not return the compliment. We had met up, we had talked, we had claimed each other as brothers, but we had never actually bothered with the usual social niceties, or even exchanged addresses. I had seen him as my brother self, but now I couldn't see him at all unless he chose to come a-visiting again. I realised that my connections with my new-found family were remarkably tenuous.

It was three days before Cain contacted me. Three days of steadily casting myself further and further adrift from the day to day world around me. I phoned in sick to work, cancelled appointments, took the phone off the hook, and now saw little point in leaving my flat unless it was to go in search of food, and most of the time, I couldn't even be bothered to do that. Instead, I wrote, chasing down ideas through labyrinths of words and losing myself in the process. I was free again and without the disturbing entanglements of other people. For a while at least, I could make everything right and as I had intended it to be. I could even subdue the growing hunger pangs, for a short while, but a confused man still has needs and mine drew me inexorably to my local supermarket.

I was in the night-drowning glare of a Tesco's car park when I found myself face to face with myself once more. He looked better than when I had seen him last, and he certainly looked better than me. There was no sign of the scarring on his face. Either he was wearing concealer, or I had been imagining things. Cain didn't come across as the sort of guy to wear make-up.

"I haven't seen you around," he said. "Are you alright?"

Ah, now there was a question. I controlled myself sufficiently to attempt an answer.

"It's not as if we normally run into one another much."

"Not into each other, but I am used to seeing you — out and about." Was that an okay response, or was I developing a touch of stalker paranoia to add to my other complaints? I just looked at him and said nothing.

"Forgive me, but you don't seem very well?"

"I'm not myself at present, if that's what you mean."

"Can I do anything to help?"

I had meant to say yes, but somehow I ended up by denying my own intentions and saying no. Whatever. It was done. I didn't feel able to unpick it. So I just stared at Cain. He stared back, face to face, mirror to mirror.

"Is it the books? Have you read them yet?"

"No. Not exactly on the top of my to do list right now. I probably ought to be reading parenting manuals instead."

"Eve's pregnant already?" I wasn't sure that I understood the "already" part of that query.

"Eve's pregnant. Yes."

"Then forget the childcare books and read the books in the library. Now. You won't understand what's taking place until you do, and Abel, you really need to understand."

"So why don't you just tell me what's happening?"

"We can't talk properly without your eyes being open."

Cain veered towards poetry and gnomic utterances. I favoured the vernacular and nothing but the vernacular.

"Fuck you and your fucking books. I'm falling apart here, and you want me to read some fucking theological treatise. I don't think so, and anyway, I don't want to go back to the house and see Eve."

"The two of you have fallen out?"

"Not exactly, but…you said it. You said she plays games. She's using what's left of my head as a bloody basketball. She's taken something of mine…of ours…our mother's. I can't have that. I want it back."

"If it relates to our mother, then it's as much hers as yours, or mine."

"Bloody rubbish. That's just more of your cryptic gobbledygook. Talk straight."

Cain stared at me: not angry, but serious. His expression reminded me of the women in the photo – all of them

"You want straight. I'll give it to you straight. Read the bloody books. Eve plays games, has always played games and always will, and right now you're her pawn when you should be the king. But you, you don't even know you're on the board. Your head won't get any clearer until you read at least one of the books. You're starting to lose it. Read. Worry about Eve and the baby after you've done it, not before. They'll be time enough to worry then, but at least you'll know what you are worrying about. Read. There is a dark moon in three nights' time. Read before then. Read, Abel, read. Is that straight enough for you?"

I nodded. He nodded in acknowledgement, turned around and walked away from me without even once looking back. Just like Eve. In the past, I would have made some clever remark, if only to myself, about not getting the hang of families. This time I just felt ignorant and alone.

XXIII

A day or so passed. I couldn't tell precisely how many: more than one I think, probably less than three. I was having problems keeping track of time. I was having problems.

The dreams had returned — the terrifying variety that involved falling into eternity. I woke up dripping with fear. I tried not to sleep, but, as I had also given up on eating regularly, I needed more rest, not less, and my situation wasn't exactly improving either my physical or mental well being. When I looked into a mirror, which I had taken to doing quite often, I saw the haggard face I had seen looking back at me when Cain had visited on the night of the full moon. Other than the absence of a scar, it was one and the same. Weight loss and lack of sleep had carved hollows and lines into my features as deeply, if far more swiftly, than water carves stone. Every time I stared into a mirror, my brother, not I, stared back. Sometimes, it even ceased to be a mirror, but became a shop window or a bookcase door, especially a bookcase door. "Read," he had said, but I hadn't. The books were still waiting.

There was no word from Eve, no further words from Cain, just my endlessly jumbled thoughts and the dreams, which, because I was resisting sleep, rapidly became waking hallucinations. Voices, speaking to me from within my head, demanded that I read what I had written. I threw myself into revising the latest draft of the ongoing novel, believing that was what they wanted. I tried to lose myself in it. It was the only escape I could see available to me, and it seemed to meet the reiterated requirements of the voices, but apparently it didn't, because it didn't quieten them. If anything, their demands grew louder and more insistent. They were berating me for not reading what I had written, but I had no idea which aspects of my previous scribblings they so fiercely wanted me to revisit.

Their voices got louder still, and my life-long sanctuary of the written word finally crumbled under the volume of their crescendoing screams and wails. And the voices carried on swelling, joining with the memory of Cain's, demanding that I read the Books of Abel in Eve's library. I resisted. I didn't want to go back to the house and to Eve. The voices continued. I knew that I couldn't go on indefinitely like this, but I was scared of how it was going to end. I didn't think I could face Eve again. She had contaminated the beauty of what, for a freeze-frame instant, we had had together. Whenever I looked at her from here on in, I would only see what had been taken away from me. She had made her choice, and now I would make mine. There was no way I was going back, but there was no way the voices were giving up. The clamour just grew and became worse, and then the voices became unbearable, and suddenly there was no longer any choice, and I was on an underground train to Regents Park, standing outside Eve's house, in the library staring through the glass door into the cabinet, but seeing a face staring back at me that I no longer knew to be my own.

Then Eve was there too; not my Eve, but the fussing maternal one, exclaiming over my appearance and my apparent state of health, and calling Cain all the names under the sun for getting me in this state. I remember challenging her on that and pointing out that Cain had done nothing to me, had tried to help in his strange way, and that she was to blame. But, she was having none of it. She blamed Cain for filling my head with lies and religious claptrap and for drawing me into his biblical obsessions. She only eased off slightly when it became clear that I had no idea what she was talking about, but by then I was unsure what even I was talking about.

She sat me down in the lounge with a large glass of dark red wine and proceeded to tell me, yet again, that my brother was insane, that he had become obsessed with the family book collection and with the tale of Cain and Abel. She was petrified that he had become so obsessed he now believed he was the reincarnation of Cain and that I was a reincarnated biblical Abel. There was a very real risk he was planning to re-enact Cain's ancient slaughter of his brother. She had got it fixed in her head that he would be preparing to do it on a night when the moon had waned as far as it could: a night of the dark moon. I needed to be on the look-out for him. I needed to get away from him and from London as soon as possible.

More wine was poured into my glass as maternal Eve disconcertingly gave way to love-struck and passionate Eve, who stroked my head and told me how much she loved me and missed me, how much she needed me and how worried she was for me in the face of Cain's growing madness. The two conflicting Eves added to my distress, and I tried to pull away, but her hands slid down my body and her stroking became firmer and more insistent. It was obvious what she wanted. I couldn't help myself. I grabbed the long rope of her hair and pulled her down onto me. She bit me. I took her breast in my mouth and bit her back. She screeched, and I stuffed her hair into her mouth to keep her quiet. She wriggled, but I held her down, digging my fingers into her soft meat. She didn't complain. Her warm flesh parted beneath me. I fucked her until I had had enough and she had stopped resisting. I lay sated on the settee. Post-coitus was combining meaningfully with the wine, the effects of sustained sleep deprivation and an empty stomach. Even a hysterical Cain wielding a carving knife would not have kept my eyes open. I fell asleep in situ, on the settee.

When I woke up it was dark. One of the reading lamps in the lounge was on, but other than that, the house was in darkness and seemingly empty apart from me. I sat still for a while enjoying the unexpected peace, but it was short lived.

Remembrance of afternoon dreams, or maybe half-imagined memories, started to push up through the dark loam of my consciousness: blackness, the sensation of falling, a spreading pool of moonlight and a darker pool of fluid, the warm softness of Eve's body as it parted under me, the feel of a knife as it penetrates the resistance of flesh, the thud as a heavy object strikes the floor, and over all this, a voice instructing me to remember, to read and remember.

I didn't know what to do, but I knew I had to do something. It was a compulsion. I stood up weakly and staggered out of the lounge, across the dark hallway and into the red-carpeted library. I switched on enough reading lamps to see by, shakily extracted from the glass-fronted cabinet one of the more modern looking books written in English and started to read.

XXIV

And Cain talked with Abel his brother: and it came to pass, when they were in the field, that Cain said to Abel, 'Pass that bottle of beer, old son. I could do with a snifter before things get heavy.' They had a drink together, brother with brother. Then they came together using the old ways and words and Cain rose up with Abel his brother and made preparations to slay him so that his blood would once again and forever flow and soak into the earth and heal it.

It was, as Eve had said, quintessentially a book on a biblical theme, a twentieth century reworking, in parts, of the story of Cain and Abel, but this was clearly an apocryphal version that portrayed Abel's death as a messianic sacrifice that somehow redeemed the world. Parts of the story were also written from Abel's view point. I was muddled from wine and sleep, and I couldn't follow it at first. Lilith appeared to be the mother of Cain and Abel rather than Eve, as she was Adam's first wife, but another Lilith made an appearance as the mother of Abel's only son. Sometimes, however, the same woman was called Lily. Resonances began to shuffle through me, like lines moving through an empty station.

For something that was supposedly relatively modern, the book's language seemed overly poetic and stylised, if not downright obtuse. Indeed, the more contemporary elements seemed out of time with the rest of it, as did the apparent intrusion of other world religions as characters, or maybe it was just one person, apparently reincarnated from one life to another. The whole was not greater than the sum of its parts. From its murk, however, individual words and phrases burned out with the clear fire of starlight. The pictures it painted in my head were clearer than the story it was attempting to tell, which was piece-meal and confused, and ominously came across like some of Cain's more prophetic sounding ramblings. For all that, though, it was still a surprisingly powerful story, and the more I read, the more I came to feel that somehow I already knew this narrative, had read the story at least once before. And I don't mean the Orthodox biblical version of events, but this convoluted, more serpentine version.

I didn't get the chance to read alone for long. The voices in my head joined in, either reading along with me or telling the same story, but in different words. It was a chorus from Babel's vertiginous tower, with many tongues intoning a variety of different versions — different events, but always the same story. Even those not speaking in English; I knew they were telling the same tale, despite the fact that I couldn't translate the actual words. Somehow, they all made sense. The fundamental story as a whole made sense, though it was far from strictly biblical: Lilith's sudden unexplained departure from the elemental paradise that some called Eden, all her nameless children scattered and lost except for Cain and Abel, who were left motherless and with the weight of a creation's destiny falling on their shoulders. But this wasn't just the need to populate a new world or enact the struggle between good or evil. This was nothing less than holding creation together, now destabilised by the loss of Lilith's primal power, against the unending pressure of chaos. The story detailed their attempts to save creation's destiny and re-harness Lilith's power in order to achieve it. It was, the voices told me, my story. Lily was my mother, Cain was my brother and I, I was Abel. Eve had got it wrong, or perhaps Cain had. It wasn't Cain who was reincarnated, it was me. I knew that now. I should have seen it earlier. I was yet another reflection of Abel in an infinite series of reflections in self-opposing mirrors. I went on forever. It was all so clear to me. Finally, after years of never being sure of myself, I had been shown who my true self was and I was primal and glorious.

I heard a movement above my head, presumably someone moving about in a room upstairs. It reminded me that there were other people caught up in my story. Having made such an important discovery, I needed to share it with somebody else to make it real.

I closed the book before I had completely finished reading it. At that moment, the tale in its entirety seemed as unimportant as the actualities surrounding it. The only reality that mattered was mine and the gloriousness that I now knew embraced it. I noticed dark stains on the previously spotless pages of the book and felt a brief stab of guilt, but then that too became insubstantial against the brightness of the discovery of my true self. I was elemental, a demi-god — maybe more than that. The marks on the book were little more than empty shadows, just like everything else around me. It felt like I was the only substantial thing here. I just needed to find Eve to share the brightness of my discovery, to show her how magnificent I had become. Once she saw the true beauty of my revelation and the shiny truths I had uncovered, she would understand and, where necessary, forgive my earlier actions.

XXV

I stood there, just looking down at her. For a moment the whole world fell silent. Eve was lying on the bed in her room, an unmoving and solid shape in the half-light cast by the street lights outside the bedroom window. Everything in the room was dark; a room of shifting smoke and tinted mirrors. Objects appeared nebulous, except for myself and Eve. Her motionless body was the constant at the centre of my vision. A black stain spread out from her head like a negative halo. I hesitated, wondering what I should do. Then, there was movement. The stain rose with her as she sat up, falling into place as a dark waterfall of hair; the darkest shadow in a room of shadows.

She spoke in a high wailing voice that sounded like the distant shrieking of sirens. I had no idea what she had just said; it was just an echo of sound beating at my ears. She spoke again, but this time her voice was more recognisably her own.

"So lover, have you read the damn books at last? Have you worked out your own story yet?"

The voice was hers, but the question was more suited to Cain, though Cain had been positive in his encouragement to read the books. Eve's question carried the disinterested bitterness of practiced ennui. I opened my own mouth to share the news of my personal revelation. Except that, in the face of Eve's boredom, the voices fell silent and my glorious discovery seemed less certain, like looking down at the Everest you think you have just climbed, only to find it is a small and rickety heap of detritus, after all. The certainty of my illumination was already fading and being replaced by doubt and encroaching darkness, once more.

Eve spoke again. When I didn't reply, she came over to me and peered up into my eyes. I found myself plummeting into the two night pools of her pupils, which merged to become one dark pit into which I felt I would fall forever, except that, here I was, vertical and standing in her bedroom as she broke eye contact.

"Not so fully awake, then, but I dare say it will come. So, what did you think of the family apocrypha?"

I didn't know how to respond without confessing my dwindling delusions, that only an instant ago had seemed so real and unquestionable, but now seemed like further proof of blind mania. So, I just stood and waited for the inevitable tirade about religious garbage and Cain's unstable obsessions, whilst trying to conceal my own. I therefore wasn't expecting or prepared for Eve's next comment.

"It is amazing that anything so fantastical could contain an element of truth, isn't it? Yet, whichever of those dusty old relics you chose to read, it doesn't really matter. They all contain that same core element, even the craziest of the narratives. At the heart there is a fundamental truth. You feel it, don't you, Abel? You don't yet understand it, but you feel it, flowing through your veins, you synapses, your secret thoughts, like a hope in the dark. That's because they are all emanations of a fundamental truth, the archetype, just like we are."

The part of me which had, in the past, condemned Cain as little short of raving, heard traces of the same insanity in Eve's words. But then, hadn't I only recently been listening to my own inner psychosis? The part of me that had, equally recently, hailed myself as the incarnation of the biblical Abel pricked up its ears at the sound of possible affirmation and launched a surge of raw undiluted adrenaline around my body.

"The stories aren't real in themselves. You couldn't quote them as history. They are stories full of holes, myths and fables, fanning the fantastical to flare the underlying truth they contain, the duality of all life. Everything has its equal and opposite: good versus evil, life and death, female versus male, positive and negative, dark and light, active and passive, yin and yang, and so on for infinity. We are all inherently opposed to ourselves. Sometimes, our opposites even talk to us, and we find ourselves acting on our contradictions, whether we want to or not."

Eve paused to peer at me again. I couldn't tell what she was seeing. Her diatribe seemed headed towards some sort of faux-Jungian lecture. I had no idea where Eve was going with it, and I'd heard enough of this sort of psychological crap in the past. All I wanted was confirmation of myself, of the splendour that I had briefly wrapped myself in. I wanted those robes back, borrowed or not. The fire of delusion was burning down fast, leaving nothing but ash and emptiness, with nothing to fill it. I was in danger of becoming a void.

"Even mankind's false Gods have had their own devils, their own counter balancing demi-urge. You and Cain are two halves of an ancient, elemental whole — diametrically opposed opposites. That is why you need to stay away from him. That is why I keep trying to warn you. He is a danger to you. For Cain to be true to his own archetype, he will need to kill you: wants to kill you, even. That is the curse of this family, to embrace the truth underpinning life, and in so doing we are doomed to act out those truths. Cain's fate is to kill you; your lot is to be killed by Cain, unless you resist it. I love you, Abel, too much to let it happen, and so I have tried to keep you from both the truth and from Cain. I won't just sit back and watch you die. "

I couldn't decide if we were still dabbling in psycho-babble territory or whether Eve was seriously trying to tell me that this family believed it had mythic duties to perform. Neither made sense, but worryingly, I wanted so very much to believe that we had been chosen for something more than dull existence, that I was finding it increasingly easy to believe we had been. That would mean I had been chosen. I no longer had to be a sad, pathetic, damaged individual. I could, at last, be special and splendid; I could belong. Yet even now, I couldn't quite let myself give up on reality. Not yet. What was left of my inner sanity was trying to resist and show me the true non-entity I actually was. My mania, however, was more than happy to embrace the mythic possibilities I felt were being presented to me by Eve. Somewhere in the middle of all this, pulled from side to side and slowly but surely being torn in two, was the person I once thought I was, the resilient Abel I used to think I knew. Whoever won this psychic tug of war, he inevitably would lose, and then I would be nothing. I wasn't ready for that and the panic was starting to rise up inside me again like the froth on a too hastily poured beer.

Eve was still talking, but I wasn't listening. I could see her, standing directly in front of me, the night time waterfall of her hair staining her shoulders, but when I glanced over there was still a shadow outline lying on the bed; wrapped in the night like a nightmare and unmoving. I couldn't work out what I was seeing. The chaos that had been rising up inside me was coming closer to the surface. And closer. I gave into the panic pushing and bubbling up inside me, shoved Eve away from me and ran down the stairs, out into the reality of the world and the anonymous, concrete, matter-of-fact turmoil of a London night.

XXVI

I want to write that I wandered mournfully and soulfully around London all night, like some poignant, but heroic, Byronic figure, then saw the light, both literally and metaphorically, the very next dawn. I want to write that, and perhaps I shall, but the truth is likely to be a good deal more complicated and anyway, I still do not know what the truth really was or is.

I rushed out into the night. That I do know. I was confused, panic fuelled, in a turmoil. That's also a given. It's what happened next that I struggle with. I get images, flashes of pictures, freeze frame, still life, a kaleidoscope of memory, but nothing consistent or reliable that I can begin to attach a plausible story to.

There is water: ink black and in straight lines, like someone has taken a ruler to it and there is other water, wide, curving and heaving; undulations of night black with the fairy lights of night time London glistening on its shifting satiny surface. I am standing on a bridge looking down at the water, at some time or times, both bodies of water. A canal and a river maybe, but then what of the third memory? Water again; a hand mirror of night with a thin crescent moon reflected sharply on its flat surface until it is distorted by the impact of a large, heavy object being rolled into its concealing depths.

Memories, visions, dreams? How many nights did I actually wander for? Where did I go? These images may not be reliable. They may be telling me things I need to know; but then, they may not.

Not all the pictures are of the night. There are snatches of daylight: traffic on the Marylebone Road, Euston Station at dawn, pigeons rising in panic at St. Pancras. How many days? How many nights?

It is night time again. Kings Cross is lit up like a cheap shop front, which in a way it is. There is an exchange of cash, and I have bought myself a little comfort in a plastic bag, but the images become even more distorted after then, assuming it is after then. I am really only guessing at the chronology, or perhaps I am simply making it all up. I no longer know. I am not sure I even knew then.

Kings Cross a second time. Dusk, I think. I see it as dusk in my head, tinctured with pink, so perhaps it is actually sunset, though that is almost dusk in itself. Perhaps I should not concern myself. There is still some life in the sky, but the important thing is, I know the moon is up there watching. Perhaps she has been there all along. Looking. Just looking.

The working girls are already out and plying their trade. There is one: short, petite, long, dark hair teasing the cheeks of her arse. She reminds me of someone. There is an exchange of cash, and I have bought myself a little comfort; a respite from the nights already passed curled up on the pavement.

A cheap hotel room; in different circumstances you would call it a hostel or a doss house rather than a hotel, but hotel will do for now. At least there is a bed: dirty, crumpled sheets — a place to rest, a place to rise. Memories. Voices. I hear them talking to me. I know it's important, but I cannot hear the individual words, only feel what they say within my gut, like a splinter working its way out. I feel the resistance of flesh: fingers caught up in long black hair, tightening, pulling, tensing, the rush of release. A bed covered loosely with stained, rumpled sheets. A thick black stain spreading out from around the head on the pillow like a negative halo. Silence punctuated by a woman's scornful laughter. A dark mirror shattered by sudden gravity. A waterfall of hair: falling.

Daylight again: Kingsway maybe, or The Aldwych. Rush hour faces intent on their business until they are caught, frozen in repugnance at the sight of something, someone, careering towards them. Right now, looking backwards in search of memory, it feels like some thing, dehumanised, no longer a whole person, but who am I to say? Only the voices might know, and they're not telling. The shadows are encroaching already, creeping up from the water and pouring down with the black waterfall of hair until I am drowning in them and can no longer think — if indeed, that is what I have previously been doing.

I am hurting now, physically hurting: my head, my ribs, my legs, as if I had been running for a very long time, or had taken a beating, or had fallen head first down a long shaft of night into a pool of deep moonlight. Except there is no moon. This night is just black cover, or as black as the streets of London allow, with their permanent amber haze leaching into the purity of the dark. Regardless, I know without looking that there is no moon, at least not the big white one. I know it in the same way I know the dragging weight of the object in my arms, just before it is absorbed into the fluid darkness at my feet; just as I know that I do not want to know. I want to forget, but how can I, when I cannot even remember? I want to wind back time, so there is nothing to forget to begin with, and I can start over again with the purity of a fresh sunrise that is withheld from me and now always will be. Yet always is not that long a time. These images will fade eventually. They are not even real, no truer than a flickering cut and paste film show. An entertainment of the brain. Why shouldn't I therefore be my own editor? Make my own cuts, remove the unwanted detritus, resume the narrative flow, shape time and history to suit my own needs? Be the storyteller and not the tale. I can do this.

What took place before here was all just a dream; cannot be allowed to be more than a dream. It is time to wake up. Now, we are moving forward positively. Now, there can be progression beyond this blocked well of a story and meaningful development to its narrative flow.

Scene: night time, London, somewhere near Regents Park. A man runs out of a large, white fronted and expensive looking house, his inner turmoil clearly visible on his face. He rushes down the steps from the front door and onto the street, plunging panic stricken into the twilight reality of a London night: crowded, anonymous, concrete, matter of fact, real.

XXVII

I should like to write that I wandered poetically around the dark nameless London streets until I saw the light of day, both literally and metaphorically, but that would be a lie and the time for lies is almost over. True, I wandered without direction through certain half-deserted streets around the capital. I saw dawn rise up over the undarkening waters of the Thames and caress London with the blessing of early morning clarity, but it was a clarity that was denied me. As was so often the case before, I remained a bystander to the apparent joy of living.

Other living creatures seem to respond to morning instinctively. It is as if they automatically know what is expected of them. The daytime birds rise to meet dawn with a song already hatched in their throats. In countryside and city alike, small creatures wake up to rustle busily and joyfully through the undergrowth and the fly-tipped leftovers of humanity's daily gorging on life. I have never understood their enthusiasm. Daylight only ends up illuminating things best left discretely abandoned in the privacy of the dark. I am not a morning person at the best of times, and this particular morning I felt my division from the rest of the world like an aggressively torn out page.

Inside my skull the voices had returned and were multiplying. Some were different versions of me, whining and pleading. Some were other. I recognised the voices of both Cain and Eve as I remembered them, but there were other nameless, faceless ones. It was a full house. And I was no longer welcome in my own head. All were berating me: for reading the book, for not reading enough of the book, for failing to remain fully unknowing, for failing to know, for failing to consume knowledge and with it understanding, for failing to act, for continuing to live...

If my internal world was no longer a secure haven, the outside world was equally inhospitable. It sensed my growing separation from it. I can remember the faces, most disgusted, some fearful, of the early morning commuters confronted by the sight of me. Convinced I was drunk or drugged or both, they gave me a wide berth wherever possible and outright Christian condemnation where not.

Somewhere around Waterloo Bridge, I huddled down against a wall for a moment's respite only to find a man come up to me, bend over my body and deliver a swift sharp kick to my ribs. The guy clearly believed in the maxim of kicking a man when he was down. Or perhaps he was proactively demonstrating the age-old human fear of the "other." Maybe I just deserved it. Heaven knows I have sins enough. I lay there and took it, making no attempt to protect myself other than to tense in anticipation of the second blow, but there wasn't one. Instead, there was a brief whimper from a throat other than mine and the sound of running feet. I tensed again as I sensed someone approach me, but there was no further kicking, just a strong arm seizing firmly, but gently, my own, and hauling me to my feet.

"Hello brother. We need to get you mended," said Cain.

He lead me away from the crowds and the sirens and I followed like the proverbial little lamb, first to one of those inhospitable automated toilets where he washed my face and hands, smoothed my hair and made an attempt at tidying my clothes in some approximation of rational humankind and then to a down market café where a pint of strong coffee and a large fried breakfast were put in front of me.

"Eat first and then we'll talk."

I wasn't convinced that I wanted to engage in conversation, but I discovered I needed to eat. I easily cleared the plate and emptied the mug. Another full mug and a plate of soggy toast were placed before me. They, too, were consumed, but in a more measured way. When I looked up from the second empty plate, Cain was scrutinising me thoughtfully. As our eyes connected, I instinctively flinched, remembering the darkness of Eve's gaze and almost expecting to be falling yet again, but this time there was no plummet out of reality, just concern and a little warmth.

"I don't know how you've done it, brother, but somehow you've managed to make things worse rather than better. The reading was supposed to wake you up to reality and return you to a full understanding, but you must have given up too soon. Now you are only partially awake. You're like a sleep walker. You've achieved semi-awareness without any understanding to go with it. I hate to think what it feels like: like being torn apart and then stuck together again badly, judging by the look of you. You've been damned by what was designed to be your salvation."

I'd had enough of vague mysticism. "Fuck you" was the only response I was capable of making. People in the café glanced in my direction and then looked away again hurriedly.

Cain shrugged, stood up, and insisted I come with him. Once again, I played the docile little lamb. We went back onto the street and walked alongside the gradual undulations of the river until we found stairs that took us down onto the Thames' mud. Cain crouched down by the murky water and stared at it in silence for a while.

"The river flows in one direction, little brother, and so does time. It is possible, if very tiring, however, to swim upstream. To regain what you once knew, you need to start swimming. First though, I am going to tell you a story. I don't think you are ready to hear it. I doubt you will believe any of it. I wouldn't in your state, but I think you need to know it before you lose anymore of yourself. You are, were, both a storyteller and a receptacle for the tale. You need to have the whole of the tale inside you before you can wake up and move forward. Ideally, the story should have been in your own words. I don't have your way with them. I prefer activity to speech, but my less than lucid ramblings will have to do for now. The sooner the story is inside you, the better. Much depends on what you do with it once you accept it as truly yours. But if it is left too long in the telling, and you crack much further, there will be nothing left to contain the story. I don't want to contemplate what would happen then. So, I want you to listen and listen thoroughly to what I have to say, even if you don't understand it, and regardless of whether you believe it. You understand that much? Okay?"

"No, I'm not okay. Nothing's okay, but if you want to waste half an hour of your time telling me a fairy story about elemental powers, then I am happy to waste half an hour of my breakdown listening to it. It's the least I can do for saving me from having what's left of my brain kicked in, though it might have done me a favour."

If truth be told, I didn't have the energy to run away from Cain, and I figured that if he was going to kill me sometime soon he wouldn't have fed me so well first. The breakfast had made me full and surprisingly sleepy. The soft lapping of the brown water was quite soothing and a vast improvement on my earlier panic-fuelled progress around London. I was no longer in a hurry to go nowhere.

Cain moved over to a lump of wood protruding from the mud and sat on it, staring once more at the water lapping at his feet. The story he told was roughly this:

Existence is made up of many layers: some we are aware of, some we are not. Some of it is comprehensible to us, some of it is not. In order to make sense of this multiplicity and to reduce it to a single linear narrative, we tell stories to ourselves, directing the flow of time into a single river. The stories we tell are convincing, but not entirely real. They are an impression, an abstraction of reality, in the same way that a poem or a painting is. The trouble is that, as humans, we have come to take comfort in and believe the stories we have shaped. We see them as real life and dismiss the true reality as fantasy, if we see it at all.

To be human is to live within the story. To live, or even just see, beyond the structures of the story, is to be more than, or less than, human.

The family is many. It lives outside of the story.

Before the clock of time was wound, three of the family, a trinity of the strongest, chose to step inside the story and become part of it. The reasons for this have long been forgotten, if they were ever known, but it is fair to say that the motivation of the three was varied.

At some stage they became human, or an approximation of it, though they had existed before then, but as what? Cain was trying to explain from inside the story. I now write this within the same constraints, and there simply are not the words to describe what we were. Outside of our human existence we were, are, always will be, elemental forces, laws of existence, expressions of formulae necessary to support the creation and flow of humanity's story. See, I told you it was difficult to explain. Fundamentally we were, and then we became, and after that we continued.

The forms we three took at the start of history were varied and have adapted over the years to fit the narrative.

One chose an immortal form, but one which eventually came to resemble humanity. It was a force of activity, of doing rather than contemplating, cause and effect, of action rather than word. The immortal gathered knowledge and memory and material value, but remained constrained by his actions.

The second made little accommodation with its host environment choosing to remain as true to its original self as possible. Becoming, to humankind at least, both an angel and a demon, a harbinger of birth and death and the icy burning flames that consume the flesh in between. Her power was strongest where the rules were weakest, but even she had to remain within the rules of the story.

The third chose to embed itself deep into the story, becoming as human as possible, living and dying, but, because of what it was, returning to rebirth every generation. It was a force of contemplation, passive rather than active, choosing words over action, observation over participation and paradoxically remaining apart from the world it had immersed itself in. He was both the most limited and the freest. He embraced the story fully and wrapped himself in it for all eternity, which may not be as long as we think. He had no memory to limit or shape him and came fresh to knowledge with each new life cycle. Swaddled in life, he could not see beyond it, but was therefore free to shape it as he chose.

The energy within and of the three had to abide by the rules to maintain the rules. Life needed their energy to exist, to hold chaos at bay, but too much elemental energy for too long a time within life's construct would destroy it, returning it to chaos. For one of the three to remain fully wrapped within the story as needed, the other two had to remain on its boundaries. It was they who made sure that the one wholly within the story died and came out of it from time to time, at the appropriate time. Then he had to be returned, reborn, like the stitching that held all the pieces together. They established prompts and triggers which enabled the third, when the time was right, to see the nature of the story and know it for what it was; to enable him to be more than, or maybe less than, human when the time came. In this way, the balance had been maintained for millennia and the laws that allowed humanity to create its own story remained inviolate. This was their existence, their purpose, allegedly.

As to who the three were, wasn't that obvious? Cain, the immortal, the man of action, Lilith, half demon, half goddess, and poor, little, weak humanity loving Abel: three forces of nature locked within, or on, the peripheries of humanity. And what of Eve? I was coming to that. It was probably as clear as moonlight to everyone else, but it took some while to seep into my consciousness; there was no Eve, there was only Lilith. Lilith, Lily, Eve, three in one, and one in three, and beyond there, I wasn't ready to go, but Cain was still tugging me forward.

Lilith was her own unholy trinity: lover, mother, and timeless demon, the death crone of myth, whilst Cain and Abel were what it said on the tin: brother selves, Yin and Yang, two of the same but in opposition to one another. Do you need the whole list? Somewhere in there, you will find high priest and sacrificial lamb, sinner and sin-eater, saviour and saved, as well as executioner and martyr, murderer and victim. Each generation has had its own way of looking at these things, but which ever way I looked at it, I ended up dead. Because for the laws to be maintained and the right energies to be held in balance, for humanity to survive as humanity, Cain had to kill his brother self. Any change to this pattern would bring about the end of the world and there would never ever be another happy-ever-after in the imploding chaos that followed. So Cain said. For the world to live, I had to die a human death at the hand of my brother, whatever mother Lilith said.

* * *

Cain saw no problem in this. He noted with interest that from time to time I had seemed to struggle with the step, but for every death there was a rebirth, and the cycle continued. Where was the harm in that? I was the crucible of the future of the human race, the one who insured that the story went on by dying. My own tale would temporarily end, but would be preserved in the form of this book and in all the volumes of my story that had accumulated before. Most importantly, it would start again with the child that Eve/Lilith was carrying inside her, my child, the next me. I hadn't been ready to go there. Cain took me.

I threw up and spent a long time trying very hard not to think too much, but the images were still there: torrents of night black hair, the smooth white line of a neck, softly rounded pale breasts tipped with dark, puckered kisses, firm white yielding flanks, that tempting, shadowy patch of musky curls where the thighs meet the body and flesh yearns to meet flesh, deep down inside — moist, dark, constricting and cradling, heated by both passion and fertility's potential. I thought I had uncovered both in Eve, but not this way, not as Cain and his implied perversions would have it: lover and mother. I threw up again.

Cain sat by the water's edge, watching the Thames make its somewhat muddy journey out to the sea. I had heard enough, but Cain was not yet ready to let me go.

"I know what you're thinking."

"Do you? Do you really?"

"The same as you always do."

"Trust me, I have never thought this before. Ever."

"But you have, you are just not willing to accept it, that's all."

"You believe all this garbage?"

"I remember it."

"It's not real."

"You always say it is fanciful, but in the end, after you have tasted your own words, you accept that it is real."

"Or sick."

"Sometimes sick, though not often. But, always real. The only difference this time is what Lilith has been saying to you, perhaps doing to you."

"Such as?"

"Trying to save you."

"She doesn't normally?"

"Not usually, no."

"And I should believe you, who are promising to kill me, over Eve, who is trying to save me, why exactly?"

"It would be better if it was a question of knowing rather than belief, and for that to happen, you need to read one of the books, your books, all the way through, from cover to cover. Each time you write another of your chronicles, you bury your trigger in the words, within the pattern and flow of the story. As the circle turns, you read it, and your eyes are opened to the truth beyond this reality, to the world beyond the story, but there is no point in me telling you. You must read it for yourself, brother."

"But I've done that."

"Not all the way through, apparently, and this time it seems you need to more than most. Maybe you haven't yet come across all of the triggers. Maybe the pattern is being distorted by Lilith's little games. They have grown more wayward, and she has interfered in ways I am struggling to see. She has hidden the truth from you and denied its existence. The clues that should have led you to the truth have not been available to you, except in a very few cases, and then she has tampered with those, too. Nothing but the full pattern will open your eyes and enable you to see your destiny for real. As for why she has done that, I can only speculate. Together we can challenge her if necessary, but you will need to embrace me as your saviour, not your murderer." Like that was going to happen anytime soon, plus, Messiah complex or what?

Cain was still in lecture mode, "You can only fulfil your destiny with your eyes wide open. Once you remember, your memories will become real, your human shell will fall away, and you will see yourself for what you really are. But Lilith's games have started to dismantle you, little piece by little piece, before you are ready, and before you can hold the freed elements of yourself together."

Finally, Cain had struck a nerve, "It's Eve, not Lilith; Eve, Eve, Eve. And she loves me. She is trying to protect me, to save me from you and your perverted fantasies. She doesn't want me dead."

"Then, by saving you, she will break the circle and destroy reality. That's a very high price to pay for love, if that's what it truly is. Love is a very human emotion. You, of all of us, should know that. Lilith is the least human of the three of us. If it was you talking of love, I might believe you, but Lilith? I doubt she knows the meaning of the word."

"You're wrong, and why should I believe you, anyway? Why should I believe any of this? We both know you're mad, cracked all the way through like a dropped paving slab. Why should I agree to come and join you on your insanity trip?"

Cain paused. "Tell me, brother, who is truly able to determine where sanity ends and insanity begins? I'd be interested to know. Everything remains subjective. Maybe it is not me who is unstable. The trauma of life and death can cause instability: continuity is far more reassuring. The point is that I warned you that you would find this all very fanciful. The only way you are ever going to know the truth beyond the story is to read your story in its entirety, up to and including its conclusion. Whatever you have written opens your mind in a way that neither I nor Lilith can. Until then, we are going to go round and round in circles, because you will never believe, and your doubts will just cause you to run away from the truth."

"So why does reading work? What does it do, that you can't?"

"I don't know. The words are written by you, for you. They are part of you, but also beyond you, your link to a greater existence. Your memories remake you. Lilith and I have always found them strangely impenetrable, but they speak to you. They tell you who you really are and show you the choices you are fated to make. You have started to read one of the books, Abel. You must have some idea. Try reading the whole story. To fully comprehend the circle, you have to travel all the way around it and understand where it ends."

And there we paused. To say anything else was only to repeat what had already been said: an endless loop, like an outer circle of hell with my dark, satanic brother pushing me back down and round every time I tried to get out. I was convinced he was insane, and even if he wasn't, I felt about him as I felt about myself: no way would I trust him. So in the end there was nothing else for it, but to return the house on the edge of Regent's Park together: Cain and Abel, same as it ever was, except this time he was most definitely my keeper.

XXVIII

All was silent as I walked in. I was expecting the house to be empty. I felt, somehow, it would be, but the hall was filled with the light of a hundred burning candles and Eve was, of course, waiting for us inside. She fussed around us both as we walked through into the lounge, protesting love and relief at seeing both of us together and in one piece. But, for all her previous warnings about Cain, she showed no fear of him, and if looks could have killed, I would have gone back to being an only child there and then. Cain was unfazed by this. He seemed more in control than she was.

"He has come here to read his story, Lilith, without interference or interruption. I am here to make sure it happens this time. If you try to stop him, you will be stepping out of your own narrative. Are you willing to take the consequences of doing that?"

Eve appeared to take time to consider this. I was hoping she was going to deny the whole mad scenario and try to get Cain to see reason, but her thoughts appeared to follow the same mentally toxic flow as Cain's. I was sucked down into it behind them both.

"In certain circumstances, yes. Wouldn't you?"

Cain didn't answer immediately. Perhaps, he too, was considering, but as he was standing directly behind me, a firm grip on my arm, I couldn't see. Eventually he said,

"No. I do not have fantasies of that sort, just nightmares."

Eve's expression did not change, but her gaze shifted from Cain to me.

"I love you Abel. You are my boy. Over and over and over again, I have loved you, and I have watched you die and each time another piece of me has died with you. For a while, I forget the pain at the joy of your rebirth and the creation of another life to be shaped. Somehow, every time I have managed to stay with you that bit longer, and then my human heart has felt your next loss that bit harder. It hurts. A mother's loss. This time, I couldn't go through with it again. I wanted to keep you alive; to keep you safe from," she cast a less than loving glance back at Cain, "him. He wants to kill you, Abel. His only purpose is to kill you. I want to save you because I love you, because I don't want to see you die again. Where's the harm in that?"

It was Cain who responded. "And what about the rest of existence, Lilith? Save Abel and you break the circle of life and death and destroy everything else. You would tear down reality and cause millions upon millions to suffer for the love of one being? I know you are capable of the destruction, if not the love, but why? If you tear down this reality, you and Abel can never be together in life, because there will be no life. You will have destroyed it. The destruction would be without purpose. It would be meaningless."

"Have you learned nothing in your millennia of existence? You have become nothing but a little man, existing only in the thrust of action and the sweet moment of death, and yet you know nothing of what it is to give birth. I will create my own meaning. If I rip down, it is only to build up again. Once I am free of the straightjacket of this existence, I can do anything. If I destroy, I can also recreate. I would be the mother of my own creation. The origin of the world lies within me. In the moments before this universe totally collapses, time itself would implode, and out of that timelessness my creation would rise. Don't you want to be a god? A real trinity at last, to stand above the false tri-partite abomination that little Man has created, a true pantheon to rival those dreamed up by small peoples. The three of us would be together with the formless ones at last. All our energies combined, shaping existence without flaw or hindrance, without petty rules or limitations. All we have to do is break the cycle."

"So, the laws would remake the universe, rather than the universe making the laws?"

"Isn't it that way already? Doesn't our very existence within the finite, shape and mould the story of life? We would just be taking things to their natural conclusion. Why shouldn't we create the clay we exist to mould? We can so easily do it, Cain. Together."

Lilith's focus was once more securely fixed on Cain. I was forgotten, a by-blow to her little drama. "And what about me? I thought you were acting out of love for me."

Lilith did not even bother to look at me, let alone look abashed at my question.

"All my boys would be together again. If I save you, I can also save the formless ones from their banishment. All would come together again as it was before. We would be complete."

I had suddenly become a stranger in a wholly alien land. It was too much. I tried to move towards Eve, but Cain grabbed my arm more firmly and held me still. Eve must have seen something in the look on my face to make her soften her tone once more and repeat her now emptier sounding protestations of love, as she moved slowly towards me, staring at me unblinkingly.

"But, of all my boys, Abel, you are the one I have always loved the most. Cain was the first, but you were the best. Your brother can't stand that," she did not bother to look at Cain, "but it's true. You have my love and respect, and so he wants to destroy you. He spouts noble words about saving the cosmos, but what it all boils down to is just plain, atavistic, human jealousy. It's always been that way. These days, he wraps it all up in the niceties of dispassionate ritual and says he is maintaining life's balance, but jealousy is jealousy and murder is murder, regardless of whether you do it under the darkness of the moon or in the unforgiving light of day. I love *you*, Abel. I just want to look after you. That's all I've ever wanted."

Eve was now standing directly in front of me, and she took my free arm and started to draw me away from Cain, but Cain was not having it. He renewed his grip on my elbow, pulled me in closer towards him and suddenly swung his other arm around my neck. I felt the pressure of something cold and hard against my windpipe and then the sensation of something warm and wet starting to trickle down my throat. I was petrified. Eve merely looked interested.

"He stays with me," said Cain.

"As you wish. But, if I choose, you know I can take him from you." Eve's smile would have been enough to curdle water.

"But, that's rather the point, isn't it? You don't get to choose. He does."

Pinioned by my brother with a knife at my throat, I didn't feel as if I had much choice, but that didn't seem to occur to Cain.

"I carry out the blood rites each time and assist Abel in his progress around the circle, the knife at the pulsating throat, the spear in the side, but only if he chooses to allow me to do it. Without his choice, it counts for nothing. Whatever happens, Abel still has to choose."

Eve moved to my side and came up close to Cain. Stroking his cheek softly she said, "And he's absolutely going to choose to have his throat slit by you, isn't he?"

Cain suddenly shoved me hard, pushing me away from him and, with the hand he had just freed from my arm, grabbed hold of Eve and spun her slight body into exactly the same position I had just relinquished. Cain's forehead appeared to be bleeding slightly, mirroring the scratch at my throat. Eve giggled as Cain pushed the knife against the soft flesh of her neck, but it was me who Cain was staring at.

"Don't run, Abel. Just wait, please."

Run? Where was I going to run to? The two people allegedly closest to me were discussing the end of everything like other people discussed bank holiday arrangements, and my grip on the reality I thought I knew had long since slackened. So, no, I wasn't going to run, but I didn't want to stay either. Then Eve giggled inappropriately again, like it was all some monolithic joke, and I became determined to stay and see this black farce through to the end.

Eve broke the ensuing silence.

"So what, dear boy, are you going to do now? At least you could have killed Abel, but you can't kill me, so why are we nuzzling up all close like this? Do you want me for yourself?"

Cain grasped Eve tighter, but never stopped looking at me.

"You're right, Lilith, I can't kill you, but I can hurt you." He drew the knife along the surface of her throat leaving a thin, but widening, red line in its wake. Eve yelped and grabbed her throat with her free hand. The wound wasn't life threatening, but there was still a fair amount of blood flowing between Eve's fingers. This time there was, however, no change or further bleeding to Cain's scar.

"It isn't just discomfort, Lilith. Eventually I will damage this physical shell of yours sufficiently badly to incapacitate you seriously for some time. Where will that leave your power games or your ability to protect little Abel? So no, I can't kill you, but I can damage you enough to destroy your plans."

Eve writhed in his grasp and tried to scratch his face with her bloodied hand, but he slashed the knife across the back of her wrist. Eve gasped and bent forward in obvious pain.

"It will heal with time and energy and no harm done to the baby. While you are distracted with healing yourself, I will give you a choice. I can seriously incapacitate your current physical form or I can kill Abel. In both instances, I will do it now without any of the usual rituals."

As he said this, Cain dragged Eve over to the door blocking my only exit. He was clearly determined that I should not be able to enact any second thoughts about leaving. He then stuck his knife into her, deep into her thigh, and twisted it. Eve gasped again, but remained upright. She did, however, cease her violent struggling and began, instead, to writhe slowly, like a reluctant cobra being charmed back into its basket.

"If I destroy this form without due ritual, it will take you so long to create another vessel for you and the child that it'll be born before you are whole again. There will be enough dark moons for Abel and me to do as we must before then. If I destroy Abel now, at the wrong time and without benefit of choice or the right words, then who knows what will happen. It may just be as if he had made the choice, and we had performed the ritual anyway, the world is saved yet again. Or his death may be so devoid of power that it will be as if he had never died. Reality will come crashing round our ears as you have wanted, and you, of course, will still have the power to make what you will from the chaos. It's a gamble, Lilith, but it would be yours to take, and you have always liked to play. If I kill him, you might get the outcome you are hoping for, and if not, the result will be the same as if I temporarily destroy your physical form now and take Abel through the ritual while you are recovering. What have you got to lose?"

I stood transfixed like a rabbit mesmerised by the two expanding electric moons of an oncoming lorry. I was powerless to help myself or Eve. Cain had turned into a deranged psycho killer before my very eyes, and I had no idea what to do. If I went for him he might kill Eve there and then, but if I didn't make a move, he might kill her anyway. What had I got to lose? I was sick and tired of being the helpless bunny rabbit or the clueless lamb, come to that. I had had enough of being done unto. It was my turn to start doing, to spread my wings and flex my claws. If Cain could have a reverse personality, why couldn't I? I wanted my moment of bloody chaos and destruction. I lunged at him. I didn't have a plan, other than to try to get the knife off him and then stick it in him as he was sticking it in Eve. I wanted to hurt him, to pay him back for what he was doing and what he wanted to do. It was the age-old blood call of revenge, but he twisted the knife further in Eve's thigh, and it was Eve who screamed at me to stand still. I stopped dead in my tracks, once more the frozen rabbit.

A dark stain slowly spread down Eve's leg, as I remembered it spreading out from her head as she lay upstairs, unmoving on her bed. The images overlapped. I chose the one I thought gave me most hope.

Eve addressed her next comment to Cain, and it was said so calmly and matter-of-factly that it was as if she was discussing the weather, not standing bleeding profusely on her lounge carpet with a large knife still embedded in her leg.

"You'd kill him now, with no time for him to make a choice or the right words to be said?"

"Yes, if that's what you want."

"What?" I made my own heartfelt interjection, and it was Eve who snapped back at me to shut the fuck up. To Cain she simply said, "Then do it."

Cain queried her decision. "I thought you loved him?"

"Love? What's that? Kill him and have done with it. That's my choice. I've made it, now do it."

Cain fixed his eyes on me, let Eve go and walked slowly towards me, the knife, still covered in Eve's blood, in his hand. I just stood there. I could see no point in running: I had already lost everything I had to lose. Slowly he came round behind me, seized my hair in his right hand and pulled back my head, exposing my throat to the knife blade. Then, he just stood there so that the pair of us were frozen in position like a biblical tableau. I could feel something wet dripping down my neck, but whether it was my own blood, or Eve's from the knife, or just the sweat of my fear, I couldn't tell.

"What are you waiting for? Do it. Kill him." There was a note of both urgency and frustration to Eve's voice that I hadn't heard previously. It couldn't be clearer that she badly wanted me dead. Cain tensed, and I could feel the blade press more firmly into my neck. I shut my eyes and waited in the darkness for my death. Then he relaxed. He lowered his knife arm away from my throat and released his grip on me. He pointed at Eve.

"So much for the primal bonding. There she stands in all her bloody glory, your one and only love. That could have as easily been your blood. It was yours she was baying for like a hyena anticipating a kill. Now, who do you trust?"

I couldn't bring myself to answer. I could still hear a wild call for blood screeching in my ears. It was my own lust for vengeance crying out for justice in the raw: the blood of those who only moments ago had been more than willing to shed mine. But, I didn't just want their blood. I wanted their suffering too: slashing and cutting and the tearing of flesh from bone: the feeling of fingers tightening around a windpipe, of a knife penetrating the soft resistance of flesh. I listened to the cruel beauty of its song, but it grew discordant, and I heard it for what it was: a brutal hymn to chaos. I couldn't accept it was a purely human urge, it was too old and too basic a feeling to be anything other than from a source truer and deeper than human, a remnant from the time when there was no time, before this narrative had a structure. I listened to it rasping along my veins and through my synapses. I savoured the longing for total destruction and the rapture that it brings, and then I let it go. Cain was still standing, waiting for his answer.

"Does it matter?"

But I knew the answer even as I asked the question. The answer was yes, to me it did, and Lilith knew it. There was no point in further talk. Maybe after a thousand and more lifetimes, it had already been said. I would never know, but she would, and so would Cain. The call to vengeance retreated with one last faint howl and with it, Lilith's hold over me. She had denied me; had chosen my death over my life. She was no longer in a position to command my emotions, tugging and surging them like the moon pulls a high tide. For all her undoubted power, the way forward now depended on choice, my choice and, maybe, if things worked out, the three of us working together in knowledge and consent. I wasn't consenting with either of them right now and currently not even with myself, but we were in stasis, which, if you believe the books, was how things were meant to be. Provided the balance held, there was nothing further to be done until, according to the books, my death and next incarnation. Perhaps my choice was less broad than I'd hoped, but then again, by that stage, I hadn't yet read the books, just the one and part of one, at that. The saga in its entirety had yet to be told, but I was having more than enough difficulty dealing with the story I had currently found myself in.

As someone who had grown up finding solace in books, escape and hope in fantasy, this was not the ending I would have chosen. I had become master of my own anti-climax. Where was the major battle for the fate of the World, which I would fight as the hero? Instead, there were three people, on the surface of things at least, just staring at one another morosely in an excessively tasteful, if somewhat blood-splattered, lounge. Was that it? Was that all there was, and where did it leave me? Had I just won the World and the right to be slaughtered at the same time? That was not my idea of a happy ending.

Cain once again read my mood.

"The circle will need to be completed, brother, but not just yet. There is still time. The choice is still yours at the end, though I believe somehow you have already made it. Lilith will know better, but I think you have at least another six moon cycles before the baby is due. Take your freedom now. Live your life as it was for a little longer and come back to us before the start of the seventh cycle to make your final choice."

He hugged me and walked away. Another departure. Just like that. Now it was just Lilith and me. It was Eve who came up to me with her gentle eyes full of tears, but when she saw my response, it was Lilith who walked away with her head held high; abandoning me yet again.

So then there was one, which was what I was used to. Except this time, if I chose to believe the other two and what I had so far read, everything I had thought I knew had been stripped away from me. I had become a man without knowledge or beliefs or the possibility of meaningful independent actions. My life was predetermined, and I was already in the hinterland of oblivion. What could I do now that would make sense?

I walked out of the house and onto the streets of London, teeming as ever with the purposeless activity of life. There was still time to loose myself amongst the seething of humanity; just another lost soul amongst so many millions.

XXIX

Time passed, as I am told it has been doing since it started. And maybe that's right, but this time was unique to me: it was *my* time. It flowed through me, was part of me, gave me my memories and my precious moments of now, those instants you are so aware of everything, there is no room for anything else, including the next moment or the one after. Everything is so alive and sharp and immediate you can't imagine it being other.

I was intent on living life to the maximum on offer. I tore down any remaining barricades and opened myself up to every experience going. Perhaps those disjointed memories of Kings Cross and other unlabelled London snapshots belong to this now and not that one.

"Classy. I'll take it off your hands, but it'll be less for immediate cash."

"For that money, guv, you won't get a better high on this side of the Thames."

"It's cash up front, then there's this place we can go."

We went, I stayed, we fucked, and then I moved on. The city became my bed.

As to how much time had passed since I had walked out of the house, who knows? The only time that mattered to me was now.

There is, of course, at least one alternative to these snatched remembrances; proof of the duality of existence, or its duplicity. Maybe these memory pools aren't mine at all? Maybe they belong, not just to a different now, but to a different Abel? I don't know if that would be a blessing or a curse. If I could choose, which would I want: flawed, venial humanity, rolling around in its muck and confusion, or the other, a second rate saviour with a mummy fixation and a death wish?

If I believed the myth, I had no choice. I was a being outside of time to whom time was immaterial, but it didn't feel like that; I didn't feel like that. I wanted as much time for myself as possible, but time was impatient. The more I partied, the worse it became. I could feel it fretting away, and I fretted with it. Then, of course, whether I believed it or not, I knew what was supposedly waiting for me once my extended party was over.

The books were still waiting. Shelf upon shelf. All of them apparently mine. Waiting in the large, strangely silent house near the park. I had started to read one book, but it needed to be finished and the others were expecting their turn, too.

The book I had started to read had given me some knowledge, if I was prepared to accept it. I had learned how and what my predecessor thought. I had read his past, explored Cain and Eve's beliefs. I even knew some of the practice. If you are half-way bright you can know quite a lot of things on the surface without ever penetrating beneath.

The book had provided information, bright images like children's book illustrations that stuck in my head, but no more than that. It had not shown me truth. For a while, I had grandiosely thought it had, but that had faded, and now I did not know. If the pages were once memories, they belonged to someone else and not to me. They questioned, but did not answer. The promised epiphany had passed me by. This might mean that I had, in some way, failed, or that there was nothing to fail because my newly found nearest and dearest were taking me for a complex and fantastical scam. Or that, collectively, we were all just barking: a shared family psychosis. Who knew?

Trapped within the plot of my own story, how could I ever hope to comprehend what lay hidden beyond it, even if it was true and my only way into sanity? If I was insane, how could I ever tell what sanity looked like? Too many questions and no answers.

There was also a sickening and repellent question I was trying very hard not to ask, let alone answer. I had loved Eve. I may have retreated to the comfort of dispassion, but I still had the memories of dark, torrential hair and soft, moist skin, of the darkness that embraced, gripped, and enflamed. I could still see, with photographic clarity, the arch of her undressed body as she leant back and parted her legs for me, becoming my living bridge into ecstasy and oblivion. Eve was carrying my unwanted child, the price of our heat. Eve as mother, rather than lover, but it was the lover I recalled in such intimate and vivid detail.

As Eve had said, "Remembering absolutely everything must be intolerable. It'd be enough to drive you mad," but that's not where my madness lay.

Eve was younger than me. She couldn't be my mother. How could I be my own father? If this tale of rebirth was one huge incredible lie, then my lover and the mother of my child was betraying me incomprehensibly. If this was all true, then I had slept with my mother, a primal obscenity so appalling I still did not want to go there. Yet, if it is all true, that must mean Eve and I are not truly human, not even really male and female. As incest is a dirty little human sin, does it matter? Sexually unrestrained nature in the hot and rampant wild doesn't hesitate when the drumbeat of blood takes over. The thought of genetic lineage doesn't get in the way of an available fuck. It isn't natural.

This viewpoint, however, failed in any way to make me feel the slightest bit better. If I believed there must be some kind of way out of here, I had failed to find it.

Time is finite, but the blackest of human thoughts are not. They stretch on for infinity if you let them. Maybe I let them go on for too long, but what is too long when one has eternity? Except I didn't have eternity. Perhaps something did, but it wasn't me. I knew me, I remembered me, the me who was born in 1968, and abandoned on the steps of a synagogue. My memories belonged to me, accumulated throughout the thirty plus years I had walked this sorry world. The memories in the book belonged to another Abel, whose barely thirty years were very different from mine, or from those of the others who allegedly came and went before. Those others had had their own lives, their own hopes and memories. We were all separate. Maybe something did replicate itself from generation to generation. Maybe there was a bigger story. But, each of us had our own unique story, too, and I didn't want to lose mine. So what did I want? I wanted to live forever. Isn't that what everyone really wants? The irony was that a part of me might live forever, but only at the expense of my current shell, the shell that was my identity, my human self. To me, it seemed like the skin would be shedding the snake, but I am only human. What do I know?

And so the party went on: I went on, for a while longer.
"I know this place we can go."
"You can see the owls flying after dark, their wings fluttering against the night."
"So, are you interested, love? What's your story?"
More snapshots, more stories, more tales from the anonymous city: beginnings, refrains, and the occasional ragged chorus. More instances that would never become memories unless their story was told and gifted a conclusion.

Eventually it became clear what I had to do. It was an undeniable truth, a nagging in my head and gut that could not be ignored for any longer. The time to party was over. I had to create my own story so it would survive whatever came next. Part of me was resisting because it was what the others had done. I was becoming just one more in a line of sloughed off snake skins. I was following the pre-ordained cycle, not making my own uniquely personal way, but it turned out that my way was demanding I write.

Having kept journals and jottings for much of my adult existence, it proved quite easy to pull it all together to form a whole of sorts: a patchwork life. The pattern only becomes clear upon completion, but in the meantime, a few extra lines here, a paragraph or two there, and I virtually had my book with only small inconsistencies. And if they existed, it was because they had existed and were therefore real. Regard them as indicators of my truth.

What more do you want to know? What are you hoping for? Please tell me you're not still waiting for a happy ending; is that really how you see all this concluding? I awake one day from my confusion and see the truth for what it is? I save the world, become a super being and we all live happily ever after? Well, as much as it would be a neat and simple way to round off my story, it wouldn't be true. This is as much my life as it is a story: they both need a credible ending.

You are not going to get the conclusion you are hoping for: deal with it. Life is inconclusive: deal with that, too. I, however, have reached my own conclusions and as inconclusive as they are, they make sense — for me. Maybe that's all we can ever hope for.

Within the confines of my story, I have come to believe this. If I am truly some form of elemental force made flesh, then death is not an end except for my current debased humanity, which is unreal anyway, although it is ultimately this humanity I most fear losing. If I am nothing but my humanity, then I have already lost contact with the truth of this world and am truly alone. Rules have been broken which should not have been. I may have not been friends with sanity for quite some time — perhaps none of us have. Whichever way I look at it, death could be quite a blessing.

The issue of choice raises its wearisome head again. How much of this have I chosen and how much is pre-scripted? Will choices I make effect anything or anyone other than me? Who knows?

Perhaps the only sane solution is to live life as if it is yours and you have a choice, because maybe sometimes you do. Though you might never know when, exactly.

Cain has repeatedly said I have a final choice to make. He has never clearly stated what the choice is. I assume he thinks it is so obvious, there is no point in naming it out loud. Eve never mentions choices, but then, she likes making the decisions. A choice sounds good to me and there is the obvious one to be made. I like the idea of free will, however much of a lie it may actually be.

So, here we are. I still need to conclude my story for you to achieve some sort of understanding, so that you can start to feel what I have felt, without drowning in the confusion I appear to have inherited, but which ultimately is mine and mine alone.

A cat sitting on a wall does not feel sorry for itself. It just sits and admires the view whilst deciding on which side to jump down.

Having made its decision, it jumps. The colour of the flowers on one side of the wall is immaterial. If it jumps one way, it will land in their midst and flatten them. If it jumps the other way, it does not know if it will ever see them again. It doesn't lament the inevitable loss of the flowers, it just admires and jumps. I am learning to live as naturally as the cat.

I am therefore choosing to conclude this story, to give it the ending I think it deserves, which may not be the ending that others want. Before you read on, ask yourself this: when your time comes, do you seriously expect to go out on a fanfare of angelic trumpets and the arterial throbbing of satanic drums, or is your ending going to be less of a bang than a whimper?

XXX

Things are coming together. I sense their imminent conclusion.

These are amongst the last memories I shall relinquish to the page, though I am hanging onto them for now and for as long as I can. When they are gone, will there be anything left of me? Am I nothing but memory?

A pen scratching life into otherwise dead paper.

Rows and rows of books, almost without end, stretching away into the dark. A whole magnificent library. One of Man's routes to immortality; a bridge over the nightmare void of oblivion.

A lone wolf howling at the dark of the moon.

"Yowoooo."

"Ssh, it's only a dog barking." What did she know? What do any of us know?

A once thick, black pelt, a cascade of night, given up by its owner like the life she once wore. The putrefying stench of betrayal.

Candlelight flickering to the rhythm of the flashing lights beyond the locked windows. The wailing of sirens and the yowling of trapped wild animals commenting together, in an unholy chorus, on the unfolding of inconsequential human tragedies that are soon forgotten by the world.

Musky perfume mingling with the smell of expensive soap and the heady scent of freshly cut flowers.

"I love you."

A woman's happy laughter and the primal reassurance of being picked up and held, body close. The comfort of shared body heat and the soft, musty warmth of dark feathers around the neck, deep enough to sink a small balled fist into.

The hollow call of a night bird, briefly comforting in the loneliness of the otherwise silent dark.

Night-warm jasmine.

Two full harvest moons, one riding high in the sky and one in the depth of the night-black water, huge like the wide open eyes of an owl; watching, waiting, for a little while longer.

"Lilith."

XXXI

For a little while longer, I remain the storyteller as well as the tale. I choose to finish what I have begun. There will be time, so let me tell you what remains of my story.

The party is well and truly over. I have returned to the house near Regents Park. It was already familiar, but I have needed it to become as personal as home, so that walking into it and being a part of it is as automatic as breathing. I want what comes next to be as much a part of my life as what has gone before.

"Back again, boy?"

Did you know that from the upper rooms of the house you can hear the animals in the zoo: the wolves, of course and the lions, and sometimes the bigger birds of prey, including the owls?

"You don't get owls in London, silly."

Their cries keep me company on the nights when I do not sleep easy. That makes it both comforting and uncomfortable at the same time. I don't think I have mentioned the animals before, but they have always been there: an imprisoned feral chorus to the unravelling of events.

I have discovered the house does have a cellar. A little triumph of a sort: I knew it had to. It is hidden discreetly behind the surgical surfaces of the kitchen which Lilith's formless ones keep so clean. Press one cupboard door in just the right spot, and it opens to reveal steps down to a deep, dry cellar which pre-dates the house.

But the cellar will keep for a little while longer.

Most of my increasingly precious time has passed away in the library, where I can now see the portrait of Lily in her dark blue dress hanging brazenly on the wall. Now I have her for real, she makes me feel safer and more certain. Proof, at last, that she exists beyond my imagination. She is actual, not the first sign of a mental implosion.

"Who is able to determine where sanity ends and insanity begins?"

I have retrieved the book I had previously been reading, the one on whose pages I at least left my physical imprint, and have read it again from the beginning. This time the words made more sense. They are sharper and more bitter, like the taste of blood. The images they summon are brighter and clearer than the first time, but also harsher. There is nowhere left to hide from them, though if the truth be admitted, that is what I really want to do. I am always destined to be the rabbit or the lamb.

By its end, the story was seared into me like a ritual brand. The words felt as if they were burning with an ancient fire, which stuck and never stopped burning. The pain felt real. It left its marks, but yet it remained superficial, external to my thoughts. The real purpose of the book was to burn open my eyes from the inside and bring me to a full understanding as natural and automatic as breathing: my awakening in this pass of the cycle. My inner consciousness seems untouched by the process, however. Cain and Eve saw me reading and think I have now experienced my epiphany. I have not got around to disillusioning them.

I haven't just read one book. I have been reading my way through all the unimaginatively, if accurately, titled Books of Abel. Rows and rows of them. It has been hard going, but I feel I have come to understand them, even those not written in English, whose words flaunt their secrets at me in Greek, Latin, and what I believe is Aramaic, as well as some languages I can't identify. Maybe it is a form of osmosis or maybe it is just self-deception, but I feel I know them all.

"Myths and fables, fanning the fantastical."

Lilith has said I have written each and every one as a message to you, my future selves, and I keep any doubts on this score to myself. My past selves did not know what I know, did not feel what I feel, do not appear to have had my doubts. There are also problems with the chronology. There are gaps in the story. Not every generation seems to have produced its sacrificial lamb, or if it has, he has not written his story like the others. Perhaps the missing ones exercised their choice not to write. Perhaps not every lamb has walked voluntarily to the butcher's slab. Maybe some grew claws and wings to reveal an even deeper, truer self before they went, not gently, into the dark of the moon. Cain and Lilith do not mention this, although they claim to remember each sacrifice made. They say it is these deaths that keep the world stitched together and hold raw chaos at bay; that each death is important and that is why they remember. They are the sum of their memories. I am the sum of mine. We are now very different, even if we were once very similar. I come to this fresh, which may or may not be the point.

And now I am concluding my own book for real. I always knew I would write this version of the story, taking my jottings and turning them into a coherent whole, whilst giving them an appropriate ending in the limited time left to me.

"I carry my story with me at all times. You have to write yours as you go along."

I even knew how I would begin my story. It would begin with love, a mother's love for her child as she watches over him in his sleep.

But now the writing is almost done. The cellar is calling.

Down in the cellar Cain and Eve become their true selves. I can see no difference from their untrue ones, except it involves a series of complicated rituals which I choose not to detail here. Read the other Books of Abel if you want arcane. This is my book. This is about me and where I have come from. It is moulded from my memories and written in a way that makes sense to me. Cain and Eve perform their lengthy rituals and consider themselves transformed. I still see them as they were, but they whisper that is perfectly normal because of who and how I am.

"To fully comprehend the circle you have to travel all the way around it and understand where it ends."

Sometime, very soon, there will be three of us participating in one of their rituals. I have made my choice, you see. I have chosen to join them. They have told me I have been there many times before, but

I cannot remember. I sense that much blood has flowed there over the years. The stains have seeped into the stone and into the earth beneath, as well as into the pages of the books. It calls to me, adding its voice to the continuing chorus in my head, but I have never answered the blood cry for vengeance I first heard in this house. I block my ears to its pulsating song, with its essence of enticing depravity, and choose to live in the human word rather than the primal act.

Cain assures me the conclusion of the ritual is quick; the knife is very sharp, and he has considerable experience with it. The blade will wipe away my sins and let me start afresh. After he has done what he must do, it will be like an overpowering weariness pulling me down into the dark. Their contrasting voices assure me it will only be a few months before I return, released from the dark back into the light, cleansed, refreshed, and ready to begin again. Whoever or whatever is born, though, will not have my memories; will not share my fears or my hopes.

The books all say that Lilith's power rides with the darker moon, not the bleached and swollen monster we take for granted. Her power flows in opposition to that; further proof of the duality that underpins all life. She is strongest when the white giant is dark and the little known darker moon is in the ascendant. She claims to go flying then, but I have yet to witness it. I do remember the owl though, sitting on my cot and encouraging me to fall into the dark.

At the next dark moon I will walk down the steps into the cellar and the deeper dark that waits there, for what may be the last time as far as I am aware. If you know different, if you are able to recall some of my memories from the dark place to which they are going, then maybe I have made the right choice. Even if you can't remember, it may still be the right choice. I may get to be the hero for once, one way or another.

Have I told you yet that tonight is the first night of the dark moon? No? I would have thought you would have known. Oh well, so be it. I have already lit the candles in readiness. They line the descending steps like a military escort, rows and rows of them, lighting the way down to the blackness at the bottom.

"You dream of candles."

Tonight I shall fulfil my childhood dream and fall into the eyes of the owl, and by so doing, shall either save the world or myself: possibly.

There is little more to say. London is already singing its night-time songs: the wail of sirens seems particularly loud this evening. What I have left out, you can read for yourself elsewhere, in other books, maybe. If it is not there, it is unimportant or personal, and perhaps both. I have made my choice. I cannot believe in the triple godhead that Lilith hymns so loudly, and even if it were possible, would it be right? The three of us like gods, or maybe just the one, if one day Lilith gets to sacrifice the world rather than me. At best, we would be a disinterested deity, ineffable and uncomprehending, and what would be the point in that? Just look at the three of us: living amongst humanity for innumerable disengaged lifetimes, but always strangers to it. None of us really belong, not even to ourselves. But this time, I intend to claim me as I am, as I know me to be. I shall die a human, with human fears and doubts. That is a choice I do not think Cain or Lilith understand. But then, that is their loss as, in a wholly different way, it will be mine. It may, however, be this world's gain.

If you are reading this, then reality has not unfolded and life continues to continue, yet again. Circles have turned once more, and the moons follow their own ancient path, turn and turn about. Isn't that enough for you? It is enough for me — to be true to my story as I have told it, to enter oblivion without the raw depravity of blood on my conscience, and with the soft lullaby of the owls in my ears.

"Lilith."

About the Author

Photo credit: Colin Clark

J.S.Watts was born and grew up in London, England, and now lives and writes in East Anglia in the UK. In between, she read English at Somerville College, Oxford and spent many years working in the British education sector. She remains committed to the ideals of further and higher education despite governments of assorted political persuasions apparently trying to demolish them.

Her poetry, short stories and book reviews appear in a range of publications in Britain, Canada, Australia and the States including *Acumen, Brittle Star, Envoi, Hand + Star, Mslexia* and *Orbis* and have been broadcast on BBC and independent Radio. She has been Poetry Reviews Editor for *Open Wide Magazine* and, for a brief while, Poetry Editor for *Ethereal Tales*. Her debut poetry collection, "Cats and Other Myths" and a subsequent poetry pamphlet, "Songs of Steelyard Sue" are published by Lapwing Publications. She has read and performed all over the UK, including the Edinburgh Fringe Festival.

CPSIA information can be obtained at www.ICGtesting.com
Printed in the USA
LVOW08s0456110716

495800LV00001B/24/P